Michele

MARK HOBER

BIG NOSE BOOKS

- FOR MICHELE -

Although I never truly knew you,

you are forever in my memories.

Special thanks to John and Austa

for letting me write this story about

their beautful daughter.

Table of Contents

CHAPTER 1

The Little Paisan

I grew up during the seventies when everyone dressed in drab autumn colors, and peace signs and rainbows represented the sentiment of the time.

Our home was safely tucked into a southwest suburb of the burgeoning Silicon Valley, away from the buzzing expressways and shiny black buildings people were frenetically pushing in and out of each day. The tech boom was just in its infancy but it was quickly paving over where cherry trees and almond orchards once blossomed in abundance.

My parents bought our house with all their savings and created a cozy space amongst a neighborhood of identical pocket homes each painted a different color. Ours was a forest green and it made me smile every time we rattled into the driveway in our VW bus. It was comfortable and worn in with our daily routines.

My parents had tacked pictures of my brother, sister and I to every square inch of wall space, and exhibited our sparse trophies on the mantle above the fireplace. I loved falling asleep at night hearing the baritone voices droning from the TV in the living room and listening to my parents chat about the neighborhood gossip. They would sip coffee as my dad entertained my mom with funny anecdotes from his day. She would make tiny gasps for air as she chuckled at him, then smack his leg, telling him to stop.

I knew the names and stories of most families within a five-block radius of our home, and I could safely ride my bike down the center of the road, dodging the big sticky balls from the sweetgum trees that lined the streets.

The scent of gardenia flowers and juniper bushes permeated the hot summer air when I would ride to our swim club or the local park. Kids played on the streets, drew with chalk on the driveway, and ran through sprinklers on their front lawns.

I usually hung out with a loose pack of kids and bounced from house to house, stopping just long enough to drink from a garden hose, or hork down a baloney sandwich prepared by somebody's mother. Most of the kids outside of my orbit didn't interest me but Michele was the exception to that.

She was undoubtedly the sweetest girl I had ever met and was likely my first adolescent crush. As a young boy, she was a wonderful friend that I shared a special connection with. She had a big impact on my early development and I have always been thankful she was part of my childhood.

Although my memories of her are fleeting, she likely formed the behaviors and personalities of the people I would be drawn to throughout my life. My last summer with her provided me with some of the happiest moments of my youth; those same memories simultaneously remind me of one of the biggest tragedies to impact my adolescent life.

Michele wasn't a new person in my life but in the spring of 1975, I had started to notice her more. Our families had spent countless days together since I was born. During the summers, we pretty much lived together at our local swim club, and on the weekends, our families would pack our VW vans and caravan up to the Sierras to camp and hike in the mountains. We laughed over numerous pizzas, casseroles, and the antics of our comedian fathers.

One night, we were all sitting around a campfire and Mr. Moretti was holding court while Michele sat in his lap. He was recounting the lineage of their family tree and proclaimed that Michele came from a long line of proud Italians. He said it was her Italian blood that "gave her the fire in her soul and passion in her heart!" I never saw her fire so that always confused me, but I certainly understood her passion. She had an infectious smile that imbued kindness and her giggle made me laugh every time her dad smothered her with mustached kisses. She always knew what I was thinking before I said anything and she was comfortable, confident and cool.

In mid-June, as spring faded to summer, I was enjoying my final weeks in the second grade at James Latimer elementary school. I arrived in the morning and quickly shoved my lunch into a cubby and ran out to the playground.

The best thing about my school was the playground. It had an extensive blacktop area with numerous tetherball poles and foursquare courts marked by thick white paint. Bordering one end of the blacktop was a large grass field and on the other was an enclosure of climbing structures surrounded by cedar chips. Along the back was an unremarkable strand of dirt and weeds that was rarely visited unless a loose ball rolled into the area.

The playground was already vibrant with kids running and playing games in the cool morning shadows. I reviewed the competition and found a foursquare game with one kid waiting and players I could easily dispatch.

I sat patiently on the bench waiting my turn, then bashfully entered the first square when the winner barked at me. The other kids chatted and goaded each other as I quietly, yet skillfully, progressed my way up to the server's square—the vaunted winner's position. The idea was to conquer this position and defend it without being knocked out for the entirety of recess.

I was engaged in an intense match defending my position when I was distracted by Michele's entrance to the playground. She was easy to spot because she always wore a bright red bow in her hair that held a neat ponytail in place. She sported denim overalls with a pastel green blouse and Chuck Taylor high tops. Her perpetual smile was accentuated by faint dimples.

As I glanced toward Michele, I missed the ball when it skipped across my square and was quickly exited from our match.

"You're out!" someone announced. Frustrated, I chided myself and returned to the bench.

Michele always commanded my attention, regardless of what was in my immediate vicinity. She wasn't flashy or demanding, but she had a magnetic energy that drew me in and kept my attention to the point I would find myself smiling just because I was in her presence.

As I sat waiting impatiently for "next ups," I scanned the playground to see where she had wandered. She briefly mingled with a circle of girls then broke away and walked to the "no man's" land at the rear of the playground. She was kneeling down and I had to stretch to figure out what she was doing. Once again, I was distracted and nearly hit in the head by a giant rubber ball.

"Hey, Mark!" one of the kids chirped at me.

He held his hands up. "Can you get the ball?"

I threw the ball to him then walked away. "I'm not gonna play anymore!"

He shrugged and dismissed me.

I wound my way through clumps of kids over to the grassy field and found a spot to lay down, prone on the grass. I pretended to play with a line of ants moving along the pavement while simultaneously watching Michele.

As I gathered intel, I was startled by a kick to the back of my shoe. Liam Wood had somehow escaped my attention and maneuvered around behind me. He stood directly in the early morning sunlight, thumb in mouth, blanket in hand and sprigs of tussled blonde hair shooting off in multiple directions. He had what looked like a jelly stain smeared permanently in one corner of his mouth.

My mom always referred to Liam Wood as one of my closest "friends." However, I was usually drawn to him out of a conflicted sense of duty and sympathy. I found the guy intriguing, but I certainly never considered him a close friend. Our union was due mainly to the geographic and economic convenience for our mothers more than anything else. They were in the local PTA together and shared a cheap baby sitter that my mom co-opted anytime she had a meeting to attend.

Liam provided occasional slapstick comedy but otherwise, I often felt he was more nuisance than friend.

"Hey! What're you doing?" he asked.

"Watching the ants." I pointed at a fuzzy line vibrating across the pavement.

He knelt next to me and watched the train of ants streaming by. "Where are they going?"

"They're moving food and stuff into that hole." I pointed at the ground while watching Michele as she moved back and forth to an old shed.

"Humph." Liam was unimpressed and sucked at his thumb. "Why are they bringing all that stuff to their hole?"

"They need to gather food for everyone to eat." Halfhearted, I continued our conversation, fully focused on Michele's activity.

"Let's step on them!" Liam yelled out.

I turned and glared at him. "No! They're not hurting anyone."

He shrugged and re-inserted his thumb, then kicked a piece of bark into the line of ants, creating chaos in their column.

"Why'd you do that? If you're not going to play nicely then go somewhere else!" I threw the piece of bark onto the field.

Michele glanced in my direction after my outburst. She was standing with her hands on her hips, smirking at me. "Hi guys! Come over here!"

I hesitated and examined Liam, then Michele, considering my options. He wiped his nose on his blanket and grinned at me. I jumped to my feet and quickly walked over to Michele.

Liam shuffled behind me and I glanced back, hoping he wouldn't follow.

When we reached Michele, he stopped abruptly behind me, shadowing himself from her view. She peeked around me and chuckled. "Hi, Liam!"

He waved then sprinted off toward the cacophony of kids playing on the playground. She watched him run away and I shrugged at her.

"Why were you lying on the ground over there?" she asked.

I scratched my chin. "I like to watch the ants."

"Ants?"

"Yes. They carry a bunch of stuff from around the play-ground into their hole over there." I pointed toward the grass.

Michele nodded and watched me with curiosity. "Wouldn't you rather play foursquare?"

"I guess." I considered the foursquare game I had abandoned. "What are you doing over here?" I asked.

"I'm planting flowers in my garden!" She gestured toward a neatly tended, dirt patch with a flourish. There was a long rectangular wooden box filled with dark soil outlined by miniature white fencing.

"I never come over here." I looked around, surprised that she had ventured to play in this abandoned strip of dirt and weeds.

"The teachers said I could plant a flower garden here for everyone to enjoy." Apparently, she had taken this project on as its sole founding member.

"I love to watch the flowers bloom in the spring and it will brighten this area up. See!" She pointed at dozens of brilliant flowers bursting from the garden. It was perfectly manicured and there were three uniform rows of plants stretching toward the sun.

"Yes, it's nice. Did you do this all by yourself?"

"Mostly. Sometimes Megan and Claire help, but they don't like getting dirty." She held her hands up, caked with dark soil.

"C'mon, you can help me out!" She waved me after her and marched toward the old shed.

It seemed more of a command than a request, so I dutifully followed her.

She went to the rear of the shed, moved some things around, then re-appeared with a beautiful red flowering plant.

"Tadaaah! It's called a garden mum. Isn't it pretty!" She waved her hand in front of the plant.

"I guess so."

"Smell it!" She pushed the plant into my face.

"Yes, it does smell good."

She set the plant down and began plucking small pieces of grass that were attempting to invade the garden.

As she moved around the periphery, she recited an encyclopedia of facts about each of the plants. It was entertaining to watch her work and hear the information she had acquired. I stood admiring the garden as she flitted around prodding at the soil and plucking away dead plants and weeds.

"How do you know so much about this stuff?"

"My mom taught me. We have a garden in our backyard." She picked up the Mum.

"Do you want to help me plant this one?" I cautiously scanned the playground to see if anyone was watching.

"You can dig the hole and I'll plant it." I felt somehow obligated to help her. I was also intrigued and decided it couldn't hurt to help dig a hole.

"Okay, I can do that."

"Great! Here is a trowel you can use!"

"It's a tiny shovel?"

"Yes, it's called a trowel!" She held the trowel out.

I raised my eyebrows and shrugged.

She pointed to an empty spot at the end of a row of flowers. "You can dig the hole right here. It only needs to be about this big." She held her hands up to form a circle then looked at me between her hands.

I carefully dug the hole and piled the dirt in a neat mound. She was delighted to have a new recruit for her garden.

She watched with anticipation and although I thought she would give some instructions, she stood silent as I worked. I felt awkward, like it was some sort of spiritual ceremony. When I was done, she clapped and pointed at the dirt pile next to the hole.

"Oooooh wow!" She knelt down and pulled out a long, fleshy worm. It squirmed as she held it over her face for inspection. "These guys are really good for the flowers!"

I was stunned that a girl would hold a worm that close to her face.

She put it in my hand before I had a chance to refuse. I cradled the writhing thing unsure what to do with it.

"Amazing, isn't it?" she asked me.

"Sure." I quickly threw it on the pile of dirt.

Michele removed the plant from its container and placed it in the hole, then packed dirt around it.

Staring quietly at the flowers, she beamed with pride. "Isn't it beautiful?"

I considered the plant momentarily, but realized I was watching her with fascination when she caught my gaze.

"My mom told me that every time we put something living into the ground, we give back some of the energy we take from the earth. Isn't that nice?"

I didn't actually understand what she was talking about, but she was so happy, I just stared stupidly into her eyes.

She held her dirty thumb out. "Touch my thumb with yours!"

I bumped her thumb with mine. "Peep!"

"Now we're green thumbs!" she declared. I was happy to be indoctrinated into her club.

As I admired the plant nestled in the ground, the morning bell rang and Michele gathered the tools and returned them to the shed.

"Thank you!" She waved at me and raced across the playground to her classroom.

As I waved back, Liam reappeared out of nowhere, sucking his thumb. "That's pretty."

I admired the pristine garden, then watched Michele as she ran off.

"Yes, she is." I turned and ran to class with Liam in tow.

– CHAPTER 2 –

The Steel Beast

My school was only a few blocks from our house and I was usually one of the first kids to arrive in the morning. We rushed everywhere because my mom was a consummate task master with an endless list of activities. I was jettisoned ten minutes before the bell rang and my mom would give me a carefully prepared bag lunch labeled "Marky." My name was written in cursive with a black permanent pen. I was sucking in a whiff of the pen's vapor when we pulled up to school.

"Mark, stop it!"

"I just love the smell," I grinned.

As I reached for the door, my mom reviewed a litany of reminders, punched the brakes and pecked me on the cheek. I swung the door open and raced into the bowels of Latimer elementary. The inner halls reeked of bleach and ceramic clay as I sprinted through to the playground.

When I bounded onto the blacktop, all of the foursquare games were fully occupied. I glanced around and considered my options, then saw the massive geodesic metal dome standing eerily in the early morning shade on the opposite side of the playground. Most kids dared not attempt to scale the structure at this early morning hour. It was a well-known fact that the metal was covered with a slick morning dew, which made it perilous to climb on.

Nevertheless, I charged ahead, reasoning that I was a much better climber than most kids. The top of the dome was also a perfect vantage point to view all of the playground activities, and Michele.

Knowing the dangers of this adventure, I climbed the dome slowly, taking each rung with measured caution. It took me nearly five minutes to mount with a few near misses, but I triumphantly reached the top and grinned. I surveyed the mob of children on the playground and not a single kid saw my achievement.

As I sat with arms crossed, desperately waiting for someone to notice, Michele appeared from the building. She was sporting her trademark Chuck Taylors with a red bow in her hair. I stood up on the bars, hoping she would see me.

She scanned the playground for her friends then noticed me perched atop the dome. Perplexed, she stopped momentarily, trying to understand why anyone would climb the monstrosity at this hour.

She gave me a confused smile and waved in my direction. When she did, several other kids started to take notice of me. I was so ecstatic that she had recognized my feat, I began wildly waving my hands, a crazed grin on my face.

As I waved, my left foot slipped down from the dew-covered bar supporting my weight and I was instantly sucked inward. I jolted to a stop on my midsection as one of the crossbars thrust into my groin. Shrieking in pain, I grabbed wildly at the air, searching for something to hold on to.

The remainder of my stunt proceeded in excruciatingly slow motion as the entire playground froze to witness the final, painful moments of my performance. I slumped over, then hung by my legs from the steel frame, dangling five feet above the ground. Eventually, I succumbed to the pain in my midsection and released from the bars, flopping to the ground. The entirety of my sixty-pound body thumped on the bed of cedar chips and the remaining air in my lungs was forced out.

As I lay gasping for oxygen, I heard Michele yelling my name. She was crawling through the bars, asking if I was okay, but I couldn't answer. When I opened my eyes, she was staring down at me in astonishment. Several other pairs of eyes appeared at the periphery and I could hear teachers pushing bodies aside, barking at me to check if I was okay.

Five minutes later, with the help of several children, the teachers managed to extricate me from the climbing structure. As they inspected my body for damage, they gently reminded me that I was yet another innocent victim dismantled by the cruel metal dome.

Mrs. Gilbert guided me to a bench at the edge of the playground as the group of kids slowly dissipated, whispering about my failed stunt. Liam appeared from nowhere and began plucking cedar chips from my hair.

"I can't believe you did that! That was cool! Are you okay?"

Mrs. Gilbert gave him a disapproving grimace and shooed him away. He reluctantly shuffled four feet away and observed as she began a thorough inspection.

She rotated all of my limbs and tracked her finger in front of my eyes. "Does this hurt? What about this? Watch my finger without moving your head."

Michele milled around next to Liam, waiting for a diagnosis. When she determined that I would survive, Mrs. Gilbert began a long dissertation about the dangers of climbing on playground toys or any object greater than four feet high.

Michele and Liam watched with amusement

Once Mrs. Gilbert felt that I had learned a valuable lesson, she asked Michele to escort me to the nurses' office.

"Michele is very familiar with the nurse's office and can

help you with some cold packs and bandages." She looked to Michele. "Is that okay, sweetie?"

Michele nodded and said she would be happy to.

Mrs. Gilbert then examined Liam and raised her eyebrows indicating his presence was not needed. He saluted me and said, "Good luck!" then ran off onto the playground.

"C'mon," Michele directed me.

I followed slowly behind her as she led me through the throng of kids who had returned to their activities.

"Why in the heck did you climb that thing in the morning?"

"I dunno. I just thought it would be fun." I was still in a state of shock.

"Well, you're lucky you didn't break anything!"

"I know."

The nurses' office sat on the opposite side of the play-ground and was accustomed to serving multiple customers each week. Unfortunately, the nurse didn't come in until later in the day.

Michele opened the door, exposing a strange familiarity with the office. She immediately directed me to the bench where patients sit while being treated. I sat down and she ducked behind a counter and opened a cabinet. She returned minutes later with a tube of ointment and box of bandages. I was nervous to have her put the ointment on my cuts, but she insisted I hold my arm steady while she worked.

"Don't be a baby!" she chided. "This won't hurt, I promise."

She was very careful and chatted the entire time as she applied the antibiotic and bandages.

I examined the red bow in her hair as she worked. "Why do you wear a bow in your hair?"

She felt the bow on her head and adjusted it. "Oh. It keeps my hair out of my face when I'm playing. I made this one. Do you like it?"

"Sure, it's nice. Is red your favorite color?"

"Yep! What's your favorite color?"

"Green, I guess."

"Oh! I like green too. It reminds me of all the beautiful trees in the mountains when we drive to Tahoe. So pretty."

"Yep, exactly."

She seemed to have the dexterity of a fully trained nurse. When she completed her treatment, I counted eight Band-Aids, including the one she gingerly placed on my forehead. I was glad she was there and was happy it was her instead of the nurse.

"Lay down on the bench and put this cold pack on your forehead." She held out an ice pack and motioned for me to lay down.

When I laid down, she ran back into the office and rummaged around in a metal cabinet. She reappeared with a rectangular block of wax paper and held it triumphantly over her head.

"Graham crackers!" I yelled. The graham cracker was probably the most prized snack of every kid in elementary school. I never refused a snack of any type and my cherubic little body was evidence of that.

Michele tore open the wax paper and handed me a square, then took one for herself. We sat in silence for a few moments, munching loudly on the crispy cinnamon cut-outs as voices echoed from the playground.

I watched her as she sat gazing out the window. "How do you know so much about the nurse's office?"

"I come in every once in a while when I don't feel good."

She hopped up and grabbed a stethoscope from the nurse's desk then put the ends in her ears. She held it to my chest and I froze as she listened.

"Wow! You've got a strong heartbeat!"

"Isn't that the nurse's?" I asked nervously.

"Yes. She said I can use it. Here, listen to mine."

She put the ends in my ears and held the stethoscope to her chest.

"I can't hear anything."

"Shhh! Give it a minute."

I focused on her eyes, listening intently until I heard the slow steady thump of her heart. I couldn't help but grin. "Wow...it's pretty loud! That's really your heart beating?"

"Yep. Isn't that neat?"

I made a thumping noise. "Bump. Bump. Bump."

She giggled and pulled the stethoscope from my ears and put it back on the desk. "How's your head feeling?"

"Pretty good."

She saw a pair of crutches in the corner and started swinging back and forth kicking her Chuck Taylors in the air. We laughed as she careened around the office.

"Why do you come to the nurse's office so much?"

She turned toward the window. "I get tummy aches a lot."

"Oh, I get stomach aches too. Usually after I eat too much junk food at my grandma and grandpa's house. Do you get stomach aches from junk food?"

"No. I'm not sure why it happens. I just get really tired and my stomach pounds like my heartbeat. My mom said I should come in here and lay down when it happens. The nurse is nice and she takes care of me. She gives me a cold pack and lets me lay here like you did."

"Wow that would be nice to just come in here and take naps whenever you want."

"I'd rather be out playing."

"Yeah, that makes sense."

Michele was deep in thought, watching the kids longingly on the playground.

Our silence was broken as the bell for recess rang.

Mrs. Gilbert came into the office to check on me.

"Marky, how are you feeling?"

"Better."

"I'm sure she took good care of you." She winked at Michele.

"Well then, let's get to class." Michele turned to put the crutches in the corner then ran out the door. Within minutes, we had both been absorbed into the throbbing network of children running to their classrooms.

CHAPTER 3

The Loyal Order
of Moms

My mom was close friends with Michele's mom and they seemed to spend an inordinate amount of time "visiting." I once asked my mom what a "visit" entailed since she did an awful lot of it.

"It's when two people enjoy each other's company and we like to just sit and talk. It's nice when you have a friend to share stories with."

This seemed absurd to me. "That sounds boring."

She laughed. "You'll understand when you're older."

It didn't matter. Today we were going to "visit" with Michele and her mom and I was excited to see her. The Moretti's house was awesome. They had a huge backyard with a big lawn and lots of fun toys. The edges of their lawn were bordered with colorful flowering bushes and neatly tended lemon trees where we could play "hide and seek."

As we pulled up to Michele's house, I jumped from our VW bus and ran to the front door while my mom wrestled my sister out of the car. I rang the doorbell and waited impatiently.

Mrs. Moretti answered the door and bent down to give me a hug. She was perpetually immersed in flowery perfume and gave amazing hugs. I loved her smile and hearty laugh. She was definitely one of my favorite "mom friends".

After a brief hug, I rolled out of her arms and ran down

the hall to find Michele. "Michele is out in the backyard," she yelled.

The screen door squeaked when I slid out to find Michele on the swing set, pumping steadily through the air.

"HELLOOOO." She wasn't wearing her signature ponytail so her long brown hair was streaming wildly through the air behind her. "Jump on. See if you can catch up with me!"

I grabbed one of the swings and began pumping my legs to catch up with Michele's cadence. She giggled and threw down the first challenge of the day.

"See if you can go as high as me."

I began pushing and pulling wildly until I was swinging in unison with Michele.

We kept challenging each other to go higher until the swing set creaked under our pressure. We screamed every time we reached the top, and kicked our feet as we fell back.

"See if you can jump as far as me."

On the top of my next arc, I ejected from the swing and crashed to a stop in the grass. Michele followed my lead and rolled to a stop next to me. We lay on the grass giggling and looked up at the sky.

As the clouds floated by, we pointed out shapes.

"That's a cat. That's a dog. That's a dinosaur."

"That one is Mr. Baldwin," Michele yelled. "See, it has his big nose!"

We rolled over laughing hysterically.

As we enjoyed the puffy clouds drifting across the blue canvas, I noticed Michele's thick tousle of almond brown hair sprawled out around her. It dawned on me that I'd never seen her with her hair down before.

"How come you're not wearing your red bow today?"

"I dunno. My mom was brushing my hair this morning and I decided to keep it down. I love when it's down. It's more fun that way."

She jumped up and swung her hair, pretending to be a movie star, then scanned the yard. "Let's play hide-and-seek. You stay here and close your eyes. Count to ten and don't peek."

I always followed her lead.

After counting down the required ten alligators, I began winding through the flowering shrubs to find Michele. As I approached the last bush, I saw her peek out. She tossed a lemon at me and yelled, "Boo," then ran off.

The lemon bounced from my chest, and I quickly grabbed it from the ground. I hucked it in her general direction but used a little too much gusto. Just as she peeked out, the lemon hit her squarely in the face.

She stood momentarily shocked, then doubled over crying. She covered her nose and sprinted toward the house, sobbing.

I froze behind one of the trees and heard murmured exclamations, followed by a frenzied discussion from inside the family room. Within minutes, my mom came out calling my name.

I sank down behind one of the bushes and started crying.

"Maaark? Maaark?"

My mom searched the foliage for several minutes until she found me curled up in the dirt. I was sobbing quietly, waiting for the tongue lashing I deserved.

"What's the matter Mark? Did you have a fight with Michele?"

"No."

"What happened?"

"We were playing and I threw a lemon at her."

"Why?"

"I dunno. I just did."

My mom sat perplexed.

"Well, I think you should apologize to her. It really hurt her."

"I know. I didn't mean to."

"Why don't you come in and you can tell her you're sorry?"

When she finally convinced me to apologize, I wiped my nose on my shirt sleeve and nodded. I followed her into the house where Mrs. Moretti was standing quietly. She consoled me with a hug. "How can she be so kind when I just beaned her daughter in the face with a lemon?"

"I'm sorry, Mrs. Moretti."

"I'm sure it was an accident. I think Michele is fine, but she would probably like to talk to you. It would be really nice if you could apologize to her."

"Okay." I looked down at my feet, afraid to confront Michele.

"It's fine. She's in her bedroom at the end of the hall." She motioned in that direction.

I was unsure if I should proceed.

"I'm sure she'll be happy to see you."

I wandered down the hall until l came to a door that was partially open. I gave the door a nudge and found Michele sitting on her bed, holding an ice pack to her forehead.

Her room was brightly lit with red, blue and green flowers painted on the walls. She smiled when I appeared in the doorway. Before I had a chance to say anything, she apologized to me.

"I'm sorry for throwing the lemon at you."

"I'm sorry too! I hope it didn't hurt?"

"It's not too bad." She lowered the ice pack and there was a red welt in the middle of her forehead.

"Ow. I'm really sorry. I didn't mean to throw it so hard."

"I know." She held out her thumb. I hesitated, then gave

her the silly thumb mash up.

"Peep!"

There was a Paddington Bear on the bed beside her. "He's my best friend in the world. I just love his red hat." She smothered him with a hug and told me a story about their travels together.

"I have a jet plane and we fly to his house on the other side of the world. He lives in a beautiful kingdom and we play with all of his friends. We have tea parties and ride horses all day long without ever getting tired or having tummy aches."

I didn't know what to say and stared blindly at the bear.

We sat on the floor of her room for the next half hour as she described the variety of toys and dolls that adorned her room. I enjoyed listening to her tell the intricate stories. Her eyebrows would raise then furrow, and her dimples would accentuate whenever she giggled. I decided "visiting" wasn't such a bad thing after all.

The entire time we played in her room, a gentle murmur came from a large white machine in the corner. It pushed fresh air into the room, keeping things cool and clean. The low whirring enveloped me with a sense of security.

Our moms eventually came to the door and informed us it was nap time. I hated taking naps, but Michele seemed to be getting tired and was already climbing up on her bed. I thanked her for introducing me to Paddington Bear. We agreed to bring our bears to school so they could meet and play together.

She held her thumb up and summoned me to give her the "peep" again. I begrudgingly indulged her and she grinned as we left.

On the ride home my mom asked me if I had fun playing at Michele's.

"Yes. I love playing there. Their yard is great and I love all the toys."

"That's nice and I'm glad you enjoy spending time with Michele. She is a sweet girl." She hesitated. "You just need to be gentle with her. No wrestling around, and don't throw things at her."

"What? I don't wrestle with her," I said, disgusted with the thought.

"I know, sweetie, just be careful with her."

I sat pondering her last comment. "Why do you want me to be so careful? And why does Michele always get tired?"

"Well...she has been going to doctors so they can figure out why she hasn't been feeling well. She doesn't have as much energy as you and she gets a lot of stomach aches. They want to understand what is making her feel bad."

"Can't the doctors just give her medicine to feel better?"

"They want to, but they have to figure out what's wrong first. Then they can give her the right medicine."

"How long until they figure it out?"

"I'm not sure. Hopefully not too much longer."

I sat in our van staring out the window as the world raced by. It didn't make sense to me that the doctors couldn't give Michele medicine to get better.

I was asleep by the time our VW bus rumbled into the driveway.

– CHAPTER 4 –

Peter the Shakie

On the weekends, my dad would mow the lawn and work in the yard like the army of other fathers throughout our neighborhood. He enlisted my brother and I to help by sweeping up the cut grass in the backyard while he continued in the front.

My brother handed me a dustpan while he swept the grass into it. "Hold it straight."

I dutifully held it as steady as possible.

"Okay, now go throw it in the garbage and be careful not to drop any of the grass on the pavement!" I tip-toed over, focused on every blade of grass before dumping it in the receptacle. When I turned to walk back, he was holding the end of the broom to his mouth like a microphone, singing "Kung Fu Fighting." He danced and spun around on the patio, yelling out the words.

I joined in with the imaginary audience, dancing to his performance and laughing at his antics. I started chopping at the air with him and we cavorted around on the patio for five more minutes until our dad came through the gate to the backyard.

David yelled out another verse, swinging the broom over his head, and I followed his lead.

"Wow! What's going on back here?"

"We're dancing at the disco!" We spun around to show off our moves and my dad laughed and applauded our performance.

"That's amazing! Unfortunately, we need to run to the hardware store. Something's wrong with the lawnmower and I need to get a part for it."

We boogied around the side of the house to the driveway while he loaded the lawnmower into our van.

"Alright, let's take this American Bandstand act on the road. Jump in the car and we can get going." He did a spin then danced to the driver's side door as we shimmied into the van and slid the door closed. We blasted the Volkswagen's radio all the way to the store with the windows rolled down, singing along to the music.

When we arrived, my dad found a parking space in the front and pulled in. There was a group of people gathered near the door, sitting in a circle and socializing. They all had long hair and wore very sparse, loose-fitting clothing.

When they heard us pull up with the music blaring, they turned around. One of them flashed us a peace sign and yelled out, "Alright man!" My heart immediately started pounding faster.

My dad asked if we wanted to go in and I said, "No thanks!" My brother tugged on my arm and encouraged me to go inside.

"Come on, we can play with all the light switches, it will be fun!"

"Nope! I'm staying here!" I scrutinized the group.

"Suit yourself!" He jumped out of the van and waited while my father struggled to get the lawnmower out. I sat in the driver's seat and watched as one of the men from the group jumped up and ran around to help my dad.

"Hey man, let me help you with that!" he said.

My dad was surprised but graciously accepted his help. As they lowered the machine to the ground, my dad rolled the side door shut, and the man pushed the lawnmower up to the curb for him. I could hear them talking faintly on the other side of the van, then my dad reached in his pocket and handed him money. I thought it was strange, but then the man embraced him in a hug. "Peace to you brother!" My dad thanked him, then steered the lawnmower into the store with my brother.

In my adolescence, I had named these people "Shakies." For some reason, I had conflated the name of my favorite pizza restaurant with the term hippy. I have no idea why I bestowed this moniker upon them. Although my parents assured me that Shakies were peaceful, I considered them unpredictable and dangerous.

I lurked in the van, hoping the Shakies would leave, then fell asleep for a few minutes. When I awoke, they had all moved down to another storefront and resumed their circle, nodding and gesturing toward the sky. I studied them as they carried on an animated conversation.

I crouched behind the steering wheel, assuming I was a safe distance away. After a few minutes, I got comfortable and decided to take the car on a pretend chase around town. I bounced up and down in the seat, letting out screeching noises, then turned on the blinker and leaned into the corner, turning the wheel with all of my weight.

I was enjoying my high-speed chase when the man who helped my dad with the lawnmower walked up to the window with one of the women. I hadn't noticed him and continued bouncing in the seat and screeching around corners.

"Hey brother!" he chirped.

I jumped and fell down into the crevice between the seats. As I regained my composure, I slowly crawled back behind the wheel and slunk down so that I could just barely see out of the window.

The woman studied me, turning her head to one side and tucked her hair behind her ears. She had bright blue eyes and long, flowing white hair that had dozens of small braids interlaced with daisies.

"It's okay, little boy ... we didn't mean to scare you." She had a soft voice that made me feel at ease. She pulled one of the daisies from her hair and handed it to me through the window. I examined the daisy in her hand then glanced toward the store, unsure of what to do. She smiled at me.

"It's alright, I promise. We just wanted to share nature's beauty with you, little boy." My heart was pounding as I leaned away from the window. "These flowers are God's reminder that there is love all around us."

I took the daisy from her hand.

"Isn't it beautiful?" she asked.

"Yes." My voice trailed off.

The man put his arm around her and studied me. "Hey, man, do you have a driver's license?" He smelled like a damp towel and lavender. He was wearing a vest over his bare chest and had long curly hair that ran down his back. I studied the tattoo on his arm. It said "DOC" and there was an image of a snake wrapped around a cross.

He stood, waiting patiently for an answer. My dad was a police officer and when he went to work, he wore a neatly pressed uniform with a squeaky black leather belt and a badge on his chest. I was confused why this man was asking for my driver's license because he certainly didn't dress like a police officer.

"What?" I asked.

"Do you have a license, man? To drive this car, you need a license." He laughed and winked at me, then the woman gently led him away from our car.

"You're scaring him, let's go. Be good little boy!" She smiled at me and flashed a peace sign as they walked away.

As they meandered back to the group, I moved into the passenger seat and sat quietly staring into the store. I twirled the daisy between my fingers and considered why this was how God spread love. I had seen a ton of the daisies in the field at school and hadn't considered their significance.

When my dad and brother finally came out the front door, I was relieved to get the heck out of there. As my dad lifted the lawnmower into the van, my brother clambered into the passenger seat and told me to move to the back. "You had shotgun on the way here!" He saw the flower in my hand as I stood.

"Where'd you get that?"

"Those Shakies gave it to me." I gestured toward the group of people who were now walking down the sidewalk away from the stores. They were each carrying large satchels.

"That's strange. Why did they give you a flower?" my brother asked. My dad was now listening and watching me in the rear-view mirror.

"They asked me if I had a driver's license."

"What did you tell them?" my brother asked.

"Nothing. She handed me the daisy and they walked away."

My dad chimed in, "I think they were just kidding around with you."

"Yes, I just didn't want to get in trouble for driving the car."

My dad laughed. "Don't worry. They were just being funny and as long as the car isn't moving, you can sit in the driver's seat."

When my dad pulled out of the parking lot, he turned right onto a busy street. I watched as we passed the group of

Shakies wandering down the sidewalk.

As we approached an intersection, I caught a glimpse of someone jumping from the curb in front of another car.

My dad hit the brakes and yelled out, "Oh shoot!" Several cars in the intersection screeched to a halt. People began getting out of their cars to check on the person in the street. My dad pulled our van over to the curb and told us to wait in the car. He jumped out and ran up to the intersection.

My dad knelt and spoke to a group of people that had formed around the person on the ground. They all backed away and let my dad take over. The group of Shakies ran by our car and stopped at the corner to watch the commotion. The man with long hair and a tattoo on his arm spoke to my father then knelt down next to him.

They both sat talking to the person on the ground and seemed to be trying to help. Someone ran up with a jacket and handed it to the Shakie. He put it under the person's feet.

My brother and I were glued to the front windshield and a crowd formed around them. The Shakie seemed to be doing most of the talking and was examining the person's head. After ten minutes, we heard sirens and several police cars, fire trucks, and an ambulance pulled up.

My father stood and spoke with one of the police officers for several minutes while the paramedics helped the person on the ground. The paramedics were gathering information from the Shakie and he seemed to be directing them. They finally rolled out a gurney and loaded the person into the back of the ambulance.

The Shakie walked over to my father and the police officer, and spoke with them for several minutes. Finally, they all shook hands and the man walked over to his friends who were still waiting on the curb.

My dad turned and walked back to our van. "What happened?" David yelled out. As my father put on his seat belt, he explained that there was a man waiting for the light to turn green before crossing the street. He had an epileptic seizure and fell in front of a car that was driving toward the intersection. Luckily, the car stopped just in time and didn't hit him.

David and I both sat staring at him. "How did you know what to do?"

"I don't always know what to do, but I'm trained to jump in and figure things out. It was actually that other man who knew how to help the person on the ground."

"You mean the Shakie?" I asked.

"His name is Peter. He was a very nice man. He was a medic in Vietnam and had done a lot of work helping injured people during the war. He knew the man was having a seizure and knew exactly what to do. I'm really glad he was there."

"Wow. I thought they just walked around yelling about stuff," I said.

"The hippies act differently than most of us, but they are usually nice people. They are just trying to stand up for the things they believe in."

On the drive home my brother and I sat in silence. My friends always thought it was cool that my father was a police officer, but to me he was just my dad. I kept looking up at him and found myself beaming with pride.

CHAPTER 5

A Trip to the Woods

Liam Wood was an interesting guy to say the least. His family were somewhat eccentric and even as a kid, I could tell they didn't operate like most "normal" families. Liam's dad was an engineer who worked at one of the technology companies and was rarely home. His mom was an artist of some sort and she was always working on various projects. Her name was "Gerry," which was very confusing to me.

I hated going over to Liam's house, but my mom would periodically leave me there to play while she ran errands. One afternoon, my mom had to take my sister to a doctor's appointment and dropped me off to play with Liam.

Their house smelled like stale peanut butter and jelly, and there were knick-knacks and art pieces on every inch of furniture. His mom buzzed from one art project to the next and "mothering" was usually an afterthought. The dishes in the sink overflowed and spilled onto the counter with specks of food their pet cat Tom would snack on. I'm not sure anyone actually fed Tom, nor was it clear that Tom was their cat.

Liam also had a weird habit of suddenly taking what he termed a "time out," although his definition of a time out was quite different than mine. He would abruptly halt any activity we were engaged in, hold out a hand like he was stopping traffic, then scurry to a corner and squat down. Staring intently down at his feet, he would hold his breath and his face would turn scarlet red. I knew things were progressing when he started grunting like a boar searching for a truffle. If things didn't go well, he would start moaning and rubbing the wall with his hand.

Gerry had briefed me on the appropriate protocol for these interludes. "Mark, please wait quietly while Liam takes his time outs. He needs to focus and go deep inside himself to relax his belly." She left me with the impression that if he didn't periodically take these breaks, his body would spontaneously implode.

Needless to say, I took the "time outs" seriously and stood clear for him to do his thing. It made sense to me because when he finished, he would yell, "Kaboom," and bounce up, ready to roll. He would have a ton of energy and immediately resume whatever activity we had been engaged in.

It wasn't until several years later that I came to the epiphany he was wearing a diaper at the ripe age of eight and was taking a break to squeeze out a turd. Now, every time I think of Liam Wood, I associate his name with a pasty, poop smell.

He was also allergic to everything on the planet. Grass, nuts, milk, strawberries, animal fur and apparently sports. He had an inhaler that he would whip out of his pocket when he was laughing too hard. He would take a massive hit from the little metal tube, then hold it in for a minute before letting out a gasp grinning like a Cheshire cat.

His allergy to fur prevented him from owning a dog and Tom the cat was rarely allowed inside the house. His parents bought him a snake because they felt every kid needed a companion pet, and what better animal to cuddle with than a snake? It was a boa constrictor he named Rocky after the squirrel in *Rocky and Bullwinkle.*

Liam kept the disgusting thing in a glass case in his room, equipped with a warming light that constantly bathed the interior with an orange glow. I hated staying the night because I would sleep on the ground, staring up at the eerily lit glass case all night, wondering if the snake would get out and crawl up my leg.

On this particular day, we were playing in his room and he suddenly stopped to take an albuterol hit. He bent over in front of Rocky's case and started tapping the glass with the metal tube in his hand. His mom constantly warned us not to tap on Rocky's glass or the snake would become "aggressive." I didn't have an enormous vocabulary but I knew if something became "aggressive," it probably wasn't good.

Liam locked eyes with the snake as it flicked its tongue. He continued to tap the glass as I advised him this was not a good idea. Rocky was about four feet long and pretty darn thick as far as snakes go. When he coiled up, he was very intimidating. Liam continued to tap away as I grew more anxious. When Rocky finally lifted his head, he coiled and struck at the glass. I don't understand why, but Liam thought this would be a good time to cuddle with the infuriated snake.

He took the wire frame off the top of the enclosure and reached in, quickly grabbing the snake behind its head, holding its torso in his other hand. It coiled around his arm and squeezed down. He whispered, "Awwww," as though that would calm the thing down. He then held it up to my face and the snake locked eyes with me, flicking its tongue. Liam urged me to pet it while waving it around like a hunk of playdough. There was no way I was going to pet Rocky, especially when he was pissed off.

Liam kept pleading and holding the snake out as it flicked its tongue. I slowly backed up until he had me in a corner, holding the stupid snake in my face. I finally closed my eyes and stuck my hand out to pet the gruesome thing. Just as I got close to its face, it snapped out and clamped onto my hand between my pointer and thumb.

"Aahhh!" I quickly pulled back as it recoiled and flicked its tongue at me.

Liam was dumbfounded. "Wow, I've never seen him do that!"

I dropped down in the corner, staring at the two puncture wounds in my hand, and started whimpering, "Get that thing away from me!"

He took it back to the case and slowly uncoiled each tendril of its muscular body from his arm, then placed it back in the warm enclosure. I clutched at my hand, waiting for the poison to flood my veins and slowly suffocate me.

I foolishly thought he would run to get aid from his mom before I succumbed to a slow, grisly death. Instead, he squatted in front of me, sucking his thumb and curiously staring into my eyes. He tilted his head to one side and whispered, "We can't tell my mom or she will take Rocky away. OK?"

I considered this, then squeezed my fist.

"Does it hurt? Are you having trouble breathing? Do you want my inhaler?" He held the albuterol bong out.

He watched me, fascinated, as I curled up in the corner, waiting for a slow death.

I decided I needed to get help. I jumped up, knocking him over, then ran down the hall, screaming, "Gerry, the snake bit me! The snake bit me!"

It took Gerry twenty minutes to calm me down and assure me that I wouldn't die from my wound. After she put antibiotic cream on my hand and bandaged me, she went down the hall to "speak" with Liam.

Within a minute, she started screaming my name. "Mark! Come here immediately!"

I knew the little turd pusher would blame the snake fiasco on me. I walked down the hall to find her on the floor holding Liam. He was laid out across her lap, completely lifeless.

I wondered out loud, "Did the snake get him too?" She looked at me bewildered and held up an empty baggy.

"Did you have a peanut butter sandwich in your bag?"

"Yes, I think so?"

She jumped up and ran to another room. "Hold Liam!"

I had no idea what was going on, so I searched the perimeter for the snake before sitting on the ground.

Liam's face was turning blue and he was holding his hands curled to his chest, motionless. I could hear Gerry banging around in a medicine chest down the hall.

I sat quietly next to Liam with my hand on his shoulder. His eyes were wide and his breathing labored. He was scared and I wondered if he was dying. I sat with him for two minutes while my heart coursed a sickening hot metal through my veins. I felt completely helpless and thought we should call an ambulance.

Finally, Gerry re-appeared with a massive syringe in her hand. "Help me roll him on his side!"

I sat there gazing in a stupor as she rolled him over and tugged his pants down. She pinched the skin on his thigh between her thumb and forefinger and swiftly pushed the syringe into his leg. I watched in dismay, having no idea what to expect.

After a few seconds, Liam coughed, then starting breathing heavily. His mom held him to her chest as the color slowly returned to his face. He began crying, then his mom started crying and then I started crying. We all sat there in his blue shag carpet, holding each other, weeping.

It took me almost a half hour to stop shaking. His mom held both of our hands and helped me calm down again. She chanted some sort of mantra and told me to center myself. Although odd, it actually worked to slow my heartbeat and I found myself giggling as Liam made a goofy face at me.

Gerry told me that Liam had a deadly allergy to peanuts and if he ate any food with peanuts, it would cause him to go into anaphylactic shock. Apparently, Liam had decided to eat the remainder of my PB&J sandwich, regardless of the consequences.

I wondered how something as simple as peanut butter could cause his body to convulse and become lifeless. It was my first "near death experience" and left a massive void in my gut.

I remained in a muted stupor for the remainder of the day until my mom finally picked me up. We never spoke about the snake attack again, but I swore I would never go to Liam's house in the future. Whenever my mom proposed going to his house, I would fall to the ground screaming and threaten to run away from home.

– CHAPTER 6 –

The Bear Caucus

Michele was gone from school for several weeks and didn't return until the final days before summer break. I was unaware she was coming back to school so when she appeared, I was surprised to see her.

I was on the grass eating my lunch with friends when she sauntered onto the playground. She seemed a little thinner and had replaced the bow in her hair with a bright red bucket hat, just like Paddington Bear's. I thought it was strange, but she wore it with style and it seemed to accentuate her character.

She didn't work in the garden or run around the playground anymore. She preferred to sit on a blanket with her friends at the edge of the lawn under the shade of a large maple tree.

That afternoon during recess, Michele was having a tea party with her friends Megan and Claire on her blanket. She was wearing her overalls and Paddington sat close by her side. Her friends wore pastel-colored dresses with bows in their hair, and they had matching dolls that looked oddly similar to their appearance.

I meandered over to the monkey bars, several feet from where she sat. As I pretended to swing from the bars, I eavesdropped on their conversation.

Michele feigned serving tea to Paddington and the dolls while the girls laughed at her antics. In a high-pitched voice, she pretended Paddington was having a silly conversation with the dolls. The girls were entertained by her show and laughed uncontrollably. Michele laughed at herself and lay down on the lawn, giggling with Paddington. As she sat up, her hat fell off and the other girls abruptly stopped laughing and gawked at Michele.

Her hair had thinned and there were large patches of her scalp showing. Michele noticed the girls staring and quickly put the hat back on her head. The girls hugged their dolls and sat in silence as Michele tried to carry on their conversation. It was the first time I'd seen Michele unsure of herself. She paused for a moment then held Paddington to her chest.

"I have to take medicine that makes my hair fall out," she said apologetically, waiting for a response from the girls. They slowly raised their eyes and studied her.

"Why does it make your hair fall out?" Megan asked.

"I don't know, it just does. I hate it but my parents say this is the only way I can get better, so I have to do it."

Megan nodded slowly at her. "I'm going to go play on the bars." She grabbed her doll and slowly walked away. Claire considered Michele, then took her doll and followed Megan.

Michele sat quietly holding Paddington, scanning the playground. I didn't want her to know I had been listening to their conversation and began swinging across the bars. When I jumped to the ground behind her, she turned and smiled at me through watery eyes.

"Don't fall again, Mark. You don't want to go to the nurse's office!" She wiped her eyes.

I wandered over, unsure of what to say.

"Where have you been?" I asked.

She looked up at me squinting then down at Paddington.

"I had to stay home for a while. I went to get more tests at a hospital in Texas."

"Wow, you went to Texas?"

"Yes, just for a little while."

"Well, I'm glad you're back at school."

She held up her bear. "Do you remember Paddington?"

"Yes, from when I was at your house."

"He keeps me company when I'm not feeling well."

"Oh, that's nice. You are both wearing the same hat too!"

"Yep. My mom got it for me to match Paddington's." She adjusted it to ensure it didn't fall off again.

"Didn't you say you have a bear?" she asked.

"Yes, I do. She keeps me company too."

"Why don't you bring her to school tomorrow and we can have a tea party?"

I hesitated and didn't answer.

"Well?" she asked. "It would be fun. Please!"

"Okay, I can bring her tomorrow."

She was excited for our date.

I did in fact have my own stuffed friend, "Trixie." However, her existence was kept highly confidential outside of the Hober house. I was slightly embarrassed of having a bear named Trixie at my age. In hindsight, I think my parents were more embarrassed trying to explain why their kid's comfort bear was named after a prostitute.

I had thoughtfully outfitted Trixie with one of my little sister's dresses and snapped a pair of plastic underwear around her butt. I have no explanation for this accoutrement.

Her head was oblong and oversized for her body with most of the hair worn off around the face. I had dragged her around the house since I was old enough to walk so her two giant eyes were scratched down to lifeless buttons that clung to her face. Nevertheless, this freak-show of a bear was my chosen comfort animal and it was time for Trixie and Paddington to meet.

The next day as my mom ran frantically around the house trying to prepare my siblings and I for another day at school, I marched proudly into the kitchen with Trixie tucked under one arm. It was rare that she made an appearance outside of my room for fear of the admonition I would receive from my older brother. He was sitting at the kitchen table deep into a bowl of cereal when I put my bear on the seat next to me.

"Oh no! What is that thing doing here?" He pointed his spoon at Trixie.

"I'm bringing her to school to meet Paddington!" I said proudly.

"Who?"

"Paddington, Michele's bear!"

"Oh my gosh. Are you serious? I can't believe you play with a girl! Aaaand you're bringing that ugly bear with you? Oh gawd! You are such a stupid!" He began laughing.

I examined Trixie slumped over on the chair next to me and thought about throwing her at his big, fat, dumb head. "Shut up!"

My mom came in and began wrestling with the highchair to strap my sister in while scolding us to stop fighting. I told her that David was making fun of Trixie. I pointed at the hapless bear next to me. My mom froze for a moment then slowly stood, frightened to peer over the table.

"Oh! Why do you have Trixie at the table, sweetheart?" She was careful not to hurt my feelings.

"I want her to be friends with Paddington, Michele's bear."

My mom was bewildered. She didn't want her little boy to be seen anywhere in public with this monstrosity.

"Oh, that's nice, honey. But they won't let you bring her to school. Also, I don't want you to lose her or you may never see her again."

"No, it's okay. They let Michele bring Paddington to school and I will hold her close to me all day so she won't get lost."

My brother scoffed and shook his head. "You're a dummy!"

"David, stop!" my mom yelped at my brother as she continued wrestling with the highchair. She finally got my sister in place, snapped in the tray, and scattered Cheerios around for her to graze on.

"Sweetie, I don't think it's a good idea to bring Trixie. She could get lost and that would be very sad."

"I'll be careful..." I pleaded.

My mom realized she would not win the battle in this moment, and ran off to gather the other crap required for kids at school.

"You can bring her in the car, but it's not a good idea to bring her into the school."

My brother was grinning at me, swinging his legs in enjoyment, soaking in my defeat. My sister poked at her Cheerios, pushing them around her tray. I considered Trixie and held steadfast that she would meet Paddington that day.

After my brother left for school, my mom packed the car and buckled my sister in her seat. I marched out with Trixie in my arms and could tell my mom was uncomfortable.

I knew Michele wouldn't laugh and make fun of Trixie like everyone else. She liked everything I did, all of my toys and all my acrobatics.

As we drove to school, my mom peeked in the rear-view mirror and began the process of explaining why Trixie was definitely not going to see the inside of my school. Like any good parent, she started with logic, the kind of logic that had a tragic ending for your stuffed animal if you didn't comply.

"Sweetie, I know you love Trixie and I would feel really badly if anything happened to her. She could get hurt, or lost, or the other kids might not be nice to her. I don't want you to bring her today, okay?"

Our discussion escalated over the ten-minute drive to school. She finally demanded that Trixie would not see the light of day. As we rolled up to the drop off area, I pulled open the sliding door of our VW van. I attempted to get out with Trixie but my mother yelled in frustration. Unfortunately, two other mothers walked by just as she lost her composure.

"She is staying in the car! She's losing an eye and all of her hair is falling out. I don't want her to get hurt anymore! Now get out of the car and leave her here!" My sister was strapped in the seat next to me, staring out the door, perplexed. Hearing the commotion, she started bawling.

At that moment, the two women saw my sister, then my mom, and stopped to glare at her in shock.

"You know how it is with these kids!" She winked at the women.

I finally capitulated and jumped out, throwing Trixie on the back seat. I glanced back as she slumped over, plastic underwear staring up at the sky.

That afternoon at lunchtime, I reluctantly sauntered out to the playground and found Michele sitting on the grass with Paddington on her blanket. She waved at me to join her, and I immediately felt disappointed when I saw her. I carried my lunch over and sat down without saying a word.

"What's the matter?" She could tell I wasn't happy. I admired Paddington sitting proudly with his bright red hat on, sharp black eyes and soft brown fur. He was a handsome bear, worthy of her affections.

"I wanted you and Paddington to meet my bear today but my mom said I couldn't bring her."

Michele chuckled. "Well, I can meet her some other time. We can just pretend she's here. What does she look like?"

I described a beautiful brown bear, more attractive than Trixie and conveniently changed her to a boy. His name is Ben, I told her.

"I thought you said it was a 'she'?"

I realized I had been caught in the first of what would become a long list of ill-advised fibs I deployed to impress girls later in life. I made a veiled attempt to cover up my lie. Michele let it go. She was smart enough to realize I was embarrassed of my "girl bear" and didn't want to hurt my feelings.

We sat for a while, pretending to drink tea and eat fancy English pastries. Michele usually did most of the talking but after a while, she fell quiet and gazed toward her garden. Most of the flowers had begun to fall off the plants and weeds had starting to invade her carefully tended space.

"What's the matter?" I asked.

"I haven't been able to take care of the garden and most of the plants are dying."

I hadn't checked on the garden since she had been gone. "I can take care of it for you."

She considered my offer for a minute. "Thanks, but it's almost summertime and you won't be here. I can just re-plant them next year." Her words trailed off as she focused on something else. It was the first time our conversation felt awkward. She was sad and I didn't know what to say.

"Mark, can you promise to plant the garden for me next year?"

I thought it was a strange request but wanted to say anything to make her happy. "Yes of course. I would love to."

She grabbed Paddington and hugged him. "Thank you." She held her bear out to me.

"Paddington loves to see all the flowers too!" I continued eating lunch quietly, enjoying my time with Michele. She poked at her food but didn't seem hungry.

"How come you're not eating?"

She hesitated for a minute. "I'm just not hungry." She squeezed Paddington tight to her chest.

She sat in silence for a few more minutes while I munched on apple slices. "My mom said I should tell my friends…" Her voice faded and she hesitated. "My mom said I should talk to my friends, but they think I'm weird and I really only want to tell you."

Her eyes watered in the sunlight. I was surprised by her sudden sadness and felt my throat catch as my eyes welled up.

"What's the matter?" I blurted.

"The doctors said that my sickness is very serious and I need to rest a lot. I have started to take medicine but it makes me feel sick and I can't play as much anymore." She hesitated and took a breath. "The medicine also makes my hair fall out so I wear this hat."

I was dumbfounded, wondering why doctors would make her take such horrible medicine.

"Why do they make you do that? It sounds awful."

"They said the medicine is fighting inside of me to get rid of all the bad parts. It's like the sickness is growing inside my body and the medicine is fighting to kill it."

"So, is that why you get tired and have tummy aches a lot?"

"Yes." Her voice faded.

"How long until you are better?" I asked.

"They don't know. I have to take the medicine for the next few months and then they will check to see how well it is working." I didn't know what to say and watched her as she held her sandwich to Paddington's mouth. "He can have my lunch."

My mind was blank for the remainder of the day. Michele's face, shadowed beneath her red bucket hat, stuck in my memory until I went to bed that night. As I faded off to sleep, I squeezed Trixie and was thankful for having my own bear.

– CHAPTER 7 –

Beehives and
Beauty Pageants

When the summer break began in 1975, I resumed my normal activities: going to swim practice, playing with friends, and enjoying hot summer days. I would think about Michele occasionally, but she spent most of her time at home. The only information I received was by eavesdropping on my parents' conversations.

My family maintained a frugal budget and what we didn't purchase off the sales rack in Mervyn's, my mom enjoyed creating on her Singer sewing machine. She embroidered multiple shirts with our names, and designs of smiley faces, animals and sunsets. One year, she tried her hand at crochet and made us each a different colored vest made of yarn. My dad even got a hat with Budweiser cans crocheted together in a bright orange macramé that they thought was hilarious.

My mom was constantly creating new garments or fabric "do-dads" for us to wear depending on the season. I would fall asleep at night, listening to the rhythmic hum of the sewing machine as my mom pressed against the pedal. It had a distinctive "knock-knock-knock" as it looped out another course of thread, then slowly wound to a stop. I loved to hear the machine's staccato humming. My mom would occasionally bark out an eloquent profanity then mumble to herself while she unraveled her mistake.

An unfortunate outcome of my mom's labors was the impromptu fashion shows she hosted when her friends came over for a "visit." I dreaded these gatherings because we were forced to put on our new outfits then march around the living room while a gaggle of women poked and prodded us. It was humiliating.

My mom had been working furiously for several weeks, sewing late into the night, and I knew she was working toward something big. Each night after dinner, she would excitedly show us the ensemble she had created. I got a blue shirt with whales embroidered on it and a pair of brown corduroy pants that had a peace sign on the back pocket.

My mom was very proud of her work. One evening, she announced with a flourish that her friends were coming over the following day and that she wanted us to wear the outfits she had created. My brother and I moaned in unison. My dad reminded us that we would all be sleeping in the dog's house if we didn't comply with her wishes.

Somehow, my brother managed to weasel out of that day's extravaganza. He was quite prescient in knowing when these events were coming and found a reason not to be anywhere in the vicinity. He had, however, provided me with sage advice regarding the lady's hairdos in the preceding hours before their "visit." Since he was my big brother, I regarded most of his wisdom as absolute.

My mom's friends would get "done up" for these get togethers, painting their nails, putting on makeup, and wearing their finest dresses. The most terrifying part of this beautification process was their hair. The women would spin their hair up in giant swirling tornadoes held together by volumes of VO5.

Thankfully, my brother had advised me to be very careful around their giant hairdos because killer bees lived in them.

If I got too close, they could come out and attack me with hundreds of painful stings. He had personally witnessed a similar incident occur with a young boy who was, coincidentally, my exact age. Apparently, the boy had gotten too close to his aunt's hairdo and suffered hundreds of bee stings. He slipped into a paralysis while gagging on white saliva and died a very slow, painful death. Suffice to say, my brother warned me to avoid any attempts at cuddling or hugging from these women.

My mom had gotten up early and spent the entire morning preparing for her big day. She had prepared all kinds of wonderful treats and covered the tables in our living room with cookies, candies and finger sandwiches.

As the final hour approached, I made several reconnaissance trips through the living room to figure out where the best treats were located. When my mom saw me lurking with my belly pressed against the table, she told me not to touch anything until the ladies arrived.

At 12:30, she gave me the signal to get ready.

"Marky, can you please go put on the nice clothes I made for you? The ladies will be here in a little while."

"Aw, Mom! I hate getting dressed up for them!"

She knew I was accustomed to wearing flip flops, shorts and a t-shirt throughout the summer months.

"I will let you pick out any one of the treats from the living room after you show the ladies your outfit."

"Ah jeez!" I shuffled down the hall, thinking about the table full of delicious treats.

As I pulled on my outfit, I could hear screaming and tiny feet while my mom wrestled my sister into a dress. Fortunately, my little sister was the opener. She relished the opportunity to prance around while the women giggled and cooed.

As the first guests arrived, I sat quietly on my bed trying not to "wrinkle" my clothes. I played with Big Jim, the counterfeit rip-off of G.I. Joe. I could hear murmured greetings as each lady arrived with their giant hairdos. They were all chit-chatting and probably wolfing down the best snacks.

When we were finally summoned for the fashion show, my sister made her grand entrance. There was a swell of "ooohs and aahs" as she flitted around the room in front of the audience. She reveled in their excitement for five minutes until I heard her do a final twirl to a crescendo of clapping.

"Marky, come out and show the girls your outfit!" I could hear the excitement in my mom's voice. My plan was to do one quick lap, grab some snacks, then run before the bees could get me.

I laid Big Jim on my bed, took a deep breath, and rushed out into the living room. As I entered, I was immediately ensconced in the fragrance of sixteen different perfumes. I could hear "oohs and aahs" as a menagerie of fingers pointed from an opaque ocean of colorful dresses.

I focused on the magnificent array of treats spread out across the coffee table. There were some with chocolate frosting, some with pink frosting, some with colorful sprinkles, some with jelly in the center and some had powdered sugar. I locked in on one of the treats and prepared to abscond with it after dutifully completing my presentation. However, before I could, my mom asked me to spin and show the peace sign on the rear pocket of my pants.

As I spun, I lost my balance and realized I'd gotten too close to the women. I was surrounded by knees and grabby hands poking at me. An army of beehives bobbed over my head, laughing and pecking at my clothes. I tried to escape the onslaught of hairdos but fell backwards onto the table of goodies. Chips, cookies, paper plates, fruit punch and napkins flew everywhere.

I scrambled to get up as the women grabbed for me. I crawled to the edge of the living room and sprinted down the hall, swatting at the air. I slammed the door, grabbed Big Jim, and hid under the blankets on my bed.

As I lay sobbing, I heard the door open.

"Marky? What's the matter? Are you okay? We didn't mean to scare you."

"Close the door!" I yelled.

"Sweetie, what's the matter?"

I didn't dare break the seal in my sheets. God only knows what my mom dragged in with her.

"Nothing, go away."

"I'm sorry. Did the ladies scare you?"

"No, I just don't want to get stung to death."

"What?" She waited quietly. "Did you say stung to death?"

"Yes! I'm not going back out there, no matter what."

"Why would you get stung to death?"

"Because of the bees in your hair!" She should have known better than to expose me to this horrific danger.

She tried to muffle her laughter. "Why would there be bees in my hair?"

"David told me that all your big hairdos attract bees and they can kill me."

"Sweetie, don't believe everything your brother tells you."

"All his friends say it's true."

She chuckled. "I think he might be pulling your leg, sweetie. Can I give you some of the treats or are you too afraid of my hair?"

I opened the sheet just wide enough to inspect her with one eyeball. She was holding a plate of cookies. I immediately dropped the blankets and sat up.

"Can I have those?"

"Of course you can." She brushed the hair from my face and kissed my forehead as I grabbed the plate of treats.

"Thank you." I retreated under the sheets and devoured the cookies with Big Jim by my side. She thanked me for showing her friends the clothes, then shut the door for my safety.

I passed out fifteen minutes later, mentally exhausted.

When I awoke, I could hear hushed whispers from some of the women talking in the living room. I recognized Mrs. Moretti's voice. She was talking about Michele. I got up and stood at the edge of my room.

Her voiced cracked as she spoke. "We have brought her to several hospitals in Texas that specialize in pediatric cancer. Most agree that she needs the treatment for at least two more months. They are hopeful but said they won't know if she is responding or if the treatment is working until it's finished."

One of the other mothers said something I couldn't hear, then Mrs. Moretti began sobbing.

"It makes her sick and she needs to sleep all the time. We try to get her to eat but she doesn't have any appetite. Food just makes her nauseous. We are hoping the medicine will at least stop the cancer from spreading."

There was silence as the mothers consoled her.

"She has a long road ahead and there is no telling what we might have to put her through. Thank you all for your help. We just want to make her comfortable and try to keep her as happy as possible."

I had heard of cancer and knew it was really bad, but couldn't imagine that Michele had it. I learned a few months later that my mom's "get together" was a fundraiser for Michele's treatments.

CHAPTER 8

Fabric Stores Stink

Later that month, I was dismayed to find out that we were taking a trip to The Yardstick Fabric Store. There was nothing worse than the fabric store, except maybe the dentist's office. Apparently, my mom's sewing hobby required a nonstop supply of materials.

The Yardstick was muffled and dulled the senses. It smelled like a mixture of vinegar and cardboard, and made me want to fall asleep immediately upon entering. It was an enormous store filled with dozens of women milling around, pulling, pointing, and touching the multitude of fabrics that hung from the aisles on long rectangular blocks of cardboard.

It could take my mom forty-five minutes to select all of her fabrics, then when she had seven to eight boards of material in her cart, we had to wait in a long line to speak to one of the clerks. The clerk would then unravel each board of material on a giant white counter-top while their long, painted fingernails clicked around until they had unwound enough for inspection.

My mom would cock her head to one side, stroke her chin, then slowly run the material between her thumb and forefinger. If a positive verdict was reached, the clerk's fingernails clicked around the counter while they measured out a length of fabric with a yellow measuring tape, then marked the fabric with chalked dashes. Finally, they would whip out a giant pair of silver shears from a holster on their belt and clip off the material. "Click, click, click...sheek, sheek, sheek..." A torturous process, I usually stood with my fingers plugged into my ears.

It was paramount to be on your best behavior, otherwise my mom would make us stand at the counter so she could "keep an eye on us." We would usually run off into the depths of the store, playing between the fabric racks.

When we arrived at The Yardstick that day, our mother gave us explicit instructions. "No running or yelling...and stay close by, I don't want to have to find you when it's time to leave."

My brother hated these trips as much as I did, but at least he made it sporting. As we entered the store, he announced that we were playing hide-and-seek. Ignoring my mom's instructions, he slugged my arm and yelled you're it, then tore off into the fabric. My mom yelled after him to walk, but he was already gone.

I was excited to play and dutifully counted off the required ten crocodiles before slipping away in a stiff speed walk. I weaved through the throngs of women and screaming children to the back of the store. There were hundreds of circular racks spread across the rear of the store. These were ideal multicolored hiding spots, but the racks required you to shimmy underneath to hide in the center area.

I began my search in the rear of the store, scanning below the racks for my brother's shoes. As I waddled around, searching beneath the endless racks of fabric, I was shoved from behind and fell to the ground. I looked up to see Josh, Michele's older brother, laughing at me.

"Hey. Why did you do that?" I said.

He held his hand out to help me up and apologized. "Sorry,

I didn't mean to knock you over! Where's David?"

"I dunno. I've been searching for him forever. We're playing hide and seek."

"I can find him!" He pushed by me and continued my search meandering through the racks.

I looked around to see if Michele might be nearby. "Is Michele here?" I yelled after him.

"Yep…" He was focused on finding my brother and faded into the sea of shoppers. I abandoned my search and went to find Michele.

After ten minutes, I found her standing at the front of the store with her mom who was talking to my mom. I hesitated to avoid being shackled to my mom's side for the final material cutting.

I stood slightly out of sight behind a drape of material, hoping Michele would see me. She scanned the surroundings with Paddington under one arm. I gave her a quick wave and caught her gaze. Michele said something to her mother then ran over.

"What are you doing here?" she giggled.

"I was playing hide-and-seek with my dumb brother."

"Oh fun." She was wearing her red bucket hat and smiled at me like we had just seen each other yesterday.

"Do you want to play hide and seek with me?" I asked.

"Yes, that would be great."

"Do you want to hide first?"

"Yes, I know a spot!" She giggled and promptly ran off with Paddington.

I was so excited to see Michele again, I forgot to begin my count down.

As I stood with my eyes closed, my brother bumped into me.

"What are you doing? Are you playing hide-and-seek?" He

was with Josh and they crowded around me, waiting for an answer.

"Yes, I'm playing with Michele. She just went to hide."

Josh suggested we play the game with all four of us. My brother winced at the idea then they huddled together and began whispering.

My brother agreed to the plan after some discussion. "Okay, yeah. Go hide! We'll try to find you and Michele."

I was suspicious but decided it could be more fun with four people.

Then he quickly amended our game. "But if we find you, I get to sock you in the arm as hard as I can."

Before I could object, they covered their eyes and started counting crocodiles. I sped off in a stiff walk, confident that I knew the best hiding spot in the store. I went to the front of the store where the sun beamed in through massive glass windows, illuminating all of the brightest and most expensive fabrics. I found a circular rack wrapped with bright spring colors and tucked into the center.

Most of the fabrics draped to the floor, and I could hear everyone checking out at the counters. I exhaled and slid to the ground, waiting. The floor was smooth and cool, and the fabric enveloped me in a cocoon. I leaned back against the center of the metal rack and looked up through the canopy of bright colors. The interior was muffled but I could hear the faint clicking of nails and chatter at the counters.

As I faded into a light slumber, I heard something shuffle on the opposite side of the rack. I thought maybe it was outside and held my breath to focus. As I squinted through the dark interior, I felt a gentle bump on my face and found myself staring into the eyes of Paddington bear. It startled me and I jumped banging my head on the metal interior of the rack.

"Ow," I squealed. I heard Michele's giggle.

"I'm sorry," she whispered, laughing.

My pain faded to glee, knowing she had found the same rack. I leaned into the middle where the sun streamed down and saw her bright green eyes gleaming. She cocked her head to the side.

"What are you doing in here?" I was ecstatic to see her. "This is the best place to hide. They'll never find us here."

She nodded. "I haven't seen you in forever."

"I know, not since the last week of school. Will they let you play outside now?" I hoped she was getting better.

"I've had a little more energy the last few days, so my mom said I could go with her to run errands. I get bored sitting in my house all day."

"Yes, that would be horrible. Are you getting better?"

"I've been feeling a little better this week, but the doctor says I need to keep taking the medicine. It makes me feel sick and I get really tired, so I sleep a lot."

"That's crummy. Do you have to take the medicine every day?" I asked.

"No. I take some pills each day but I also have to go to a clinic once in a while. I just sit there, and they hook tubes up to my arms to push medicine into my body."

"Wow, that sounds horrible."

She squeezed Paddington and we both gazed up through the cylinder of light through the fabric.

"The doctor said it's cancer." I was surprised that she blurted it out. We sat in silence and I fought the sudden feelings of sadness rushing through my mind. I didn't know what to say but wanted to comfort her.

"Well, I really miss you."

"I miss you too," she said, through watery eyes. She held up her thumb and said, "Peep!"

Just as I extended my thumb, I was grabbed by the feet and dragged out from under my hiding spot. I lay sprawled out in the middle of the store, still sobbing as our brothers laughed at me.

"We found you. We win."

As I lay in astonishment, my brother knelt down and slugged me in the arm. I coiled up in the center of the floor and began crying.

At this point, a cluster of moms circled around to identify whose child I was. "Is that Judy's son? Margaret, is he yours? Ginnie, is that your boy?" Finally, a hush settled over the crowd, the scissors stopped "sheeking," and the nails stopped clicking. It was perfectly silent as Michele slipped out from the other side of the rack and adjusted her red hat. She stood, meek and gaunt in the sun's light.

I could see my mom's silhouette as she bent down to help me up. "What happened, sweetie?"

I turned toward Michele. She was standing with her Paddington Bear, brilliant green eyes pooling, tears streaming down her cheeks. I was sad for many reasons and wanted to yell but couldn't find the words. I saw my brother snickering, then shouted, "David hit me!"

My mom hastily grabbed David by the elbow and told me to follow her as we pushed through the crowd toward the exit. My mom struggled to open the front door, and I glanced back and saw Michele standing with Paddington. Her mom put one arm around her daughter and watched as we were escorted away. She wiped her eyes and waved at me. I wondered when I would see her again and hoped it would be sometime soon.

— CHAPTER 9 —

Exposed to the Moon

The Y Indian Guides was an organization sponsored by the local YMCA and designed to help working class fathers develop stronger bonds with their sons. It was the less prestigious, snot-nosed little brother to the Boy Scouts. The YMCA provided nominal funding to each "tribe," which was meant to support outdoor activities like camping, hiking and canoeing.

In concept, it was a wonderful organization. However, it lacked a lot of structure and relied heavily on the creativity of the respective leaders for each "tribe." This was the perfect organization for my father and Mr. Moretti, who loved the outdoors and were not big fans of organization. They had hastily pulled together a list of their favorite camping spots and set up a regular meeting on the last Sunday of each month. Within one week, they received approval to set up the proud "Chippewa" tribe of the greater south bay in San Jose.

I absolutely loved the Y Indian Guides. We went camping at least three times each summer and only boys were allowed on the trips. My father was "Big Deer," my brother "Running Deer," and I was "Little Deer." We each wore leather vests that my mom had created from pleather with our tribe moniker emblazoned across the back. My father carved wooden deer caricatures for each of our names, which we pinned proudly to our left lapel.

We each wore a colorful headband adorned with feathers that we earned for household chores and various community philanthropies. There were no shiny merit badges or sashes, just eagle feathers, earned through hard work and worn proudly to every event. Whenever I received a feather, I would insert it in my headband and wear it home to show my mom.

My father didn't let me join the group until I was eight years old. I'm fairly certain this age minimum was arbitrarily set by our fathers because that was when most little boys could independently use the bathroom, and we could keep secrets. In fact, we relished the idea of keeping secrets from the girls in our family, namely our mothers.

It wasn't that we were doing anything bad, but some level of comradery was felt by keeping our escapades clandestine. Probably the biggest secret of the Chippewa tribe was that it was founded primarily to provide an escape to the mountains for the founding fathers to drink copious amounts of beer while telling stories around a campfire. It was a pretty ingenious scheme.

At the end of June, I was initiated into the tribe and had worked hard to earn five feathers. Some of the older boys had hundreds and I was quite envious. I was determined to obtain the most feathers possible and set my mind to doing as many chores as possible.

The only person with fewer feathers than me was Liam Wood. During our first meeting, I spied him across the circle, sitting cross legged and staring at one of his shoes. His band of feathers had clearly been sat upon. It appeared that someone ran over a pigeon and hastily shoved it on his head. I studied him for a minute and felt a twinge of pity.

My dad announced the first overnight that summer would be up near Angels Camp in the Sierras. There were around thirty of us going, including fathers and sons. The parents had arranged for us to stay in five separate cabins with bunk beds and cots. We would be sharing our cabin with Michele's brother and father.

Over the next two weeks, I counted down the days impatiently. Finally in mid-July, our big campout weekend arrived. My father had organized all of our camping gear in the garage the night before we planned to leave. The next morning, I woke up at the crack of dawn and was buzzing with excitement. I followed my father around, circling his ankles, asking how I could help. I figured I could earn more feathers and hasten our departure this way.

"Load some of this stuff into the car, and we can leave sooner!"

I pitched in and began throwing stuff in the van.

Once the car was packed, my dad announced we were ready to go and my brother and I had the usual rock-paper-scissor shootout for the shotgun seat. I lost and was relegated to the back seat, but I didn't care. All I could think about was my first Y Indian guides campout.

I gave my mother a quick hug and kiss as she bid us farewell while balancing my little sister in one arm. I jumped into the van and watched as my dad cooed at my little sister, then gave my mom a kiss and hugged her.

"Let's go," I yelped.

"Yeah, let's go, Dad," my brother chimed in. My dad turned and smirked at us, then gave my mom one last kiss on the cheek. As we backed down the driveway, my mom waved to us and reminded my father to drive carefully.

Thirty minutes into our trip, I passed out across the padded bench in the rear of our van. I didn't wake up until my dad starting barking at me. "Markle Farkle, we're almost there. Wake up!"

The scent of pine trees streamed in through the car windows as the van's drapes slapped at the windows in the breeze. Laying in the back and staring up through the windows, I watched as tall redwood shadows flitted by and we weaved our way through the mountains. It was invigorating to breathe in the cool mountain air and enjoy the kaleidoscope of forest green flashing by the windows.

My dad finally pulled off the winding road and slowed to a stop. One of the fathers was standing on the side of the road and waved to us. He walked up to my dad's window and they proceeded to talk and joke around for far too long. As I waited impatiently in the back, my brother announced that he needed to pee.

"So do I!"

My brother turned and winked at me. The man quickly gave my father directions to our cabin and gestured up the road.

My dad jolted the van forward and pointed to a group of small cottages up the road. "The cabins are just up here on the right," he announced as we pulled into a dirt parking lot facing a row of identical chocolate brown cottages. The cabins looked like they were built in the early 1900s and each had a wooden front porch that bestowed a historic "gold rush town" appeal.

"This one is ours," my dad said.

I was sliding the door open and jumping to the ground before my dad pulled on the emergency break. My brother and I raced to the front porch of the cabin and ran through a torn screen door.

Mr. Moretti stood in the middle of the cabin and met us with a booming welcome. "The Hobers are here." He demanded I give him a hug and hoisted me into his arms before I could scramble free to explore the rooms. "How are you,

Markle Farkle?" He was beaming as usual.

"I'm good, except I wish Michele could've come camping with us." I stopped for a moment and was embarrassed by my outburst in all of the excitement.

"So do I," he said. "Pretty soon, I hope." He winked at my dad who was walking through the front door carrying food. As my dad put the box on a table, Mr. Moretti gave him a quick handshake and hug.

"Can I help you out?" Mr. Moretti asked.

"Sure, we have a lot of stuff."

"Where's Josh?" my brother asked.

"He went up to the lake with some of the other boys. He should be back in a while."

My father and Mr. Moretti began carting in camping gear as my brother and I tore through the cabin. There were three bedrooms off to the sides of the main area. Each room had one bunk bed and one cot.

I ran to our room in the rear of the cabin. Each of the bunks had old bedrolls. I threw my sleeping bag on the top bunk and scrambled up the ladder to claim my spot. My brother did the same on the lower bunk.

"Fine with me, the spiders like to live in the top bunk," he said.

I surveyed the spider webs in the corners of the ceiling but decided it was worth the risk. I loved laying in the top bunk at night so I could gaze at the stars through the window.

That afternoon, we went on a short hike to a lake two miles up from our campsite. The lake was nestled within granite rocks, fed by a small stream that trickled down through the forest from melting snow further up the mountain.

The fathers chatted, enjoying the scenery while the kids explored the terrain and engaged in a rock skipping contest.

Liam sat by himself near a section of the lake that formed

a small pool in the rocks. He threw pebbles in the water with his blanket over his shoulder. I wandered over to check on him.

"What are you doing over here?"

"There are tiny fish in there, see." He pointed at the water and I could see many small minnows darting around. "Watch this." He threw a pebble in the water and the fish instantly shot to the edges.

"Yes, they're really fast." I threw a pebble in to see the reaction as the fish scattered.

He had taken the band off his head with its sole feather and thrown it on one of the rocks.

"How come you don't have more feathers?" I asked him.

He continued throwing rocks into the water. "I dunno. My dad is always at work so I can't do any projects and my mom tells me I shouldn't do chores around the house. Besides, I just like to have fun and go camping without having to do all that stuff."

I considered his pathetic headband and felt another pang of guilt.

"Well, I'll try to think of something we can both do to help you get a few more."

"Why?" He said suspiciously.

"Because it would be fun and you could get more feathers."

"I just don't really know what to do."

"We'll think of something," I said.

"Sounds good," He threw the remaining pebbles in the water, pulled his headband around his arm, and followed me back toward the group.

The dads had begun packing up and said we were heading back to our camp.

That evening, we put on our Indian Guides' garb and filed down to the dining hall for dinner. I loved wearing the headband and vest, even though I only had five feathers. The dining hall was a loud and colorful collage of people wearing feathered clothing and headdresses. There were hundreds of kids with their fathers talking about the stories from the day. Each person had a vest with patches on it that represented their tribe and awards they had received.

After filling our trays with food, my dad found our group and we sat at a table with the other families from our tribe. My dad and Mr. Moretti held court for about thirty minutes, telling jokes and stories about prior years' adventures. The other fathers seemed to be entertained by the duo but I only understood half of the funny stories they told.

After dinner, all of the tribes filed outside and gathered around an enormous campfire that climbed twenty feet into the sky. A semi-circle of benches surrounded the fire, facing down on a raised concrete area that served as a stage. People flooded in with their ceremonial costumes and found seats around the stage.

On this first night, there were several grand opening rituals emceed by a large, powerful man who resembled an Indian chief. He wore a headdress that ran from his head all the way down his back. He had painted his face and arms with red symbols, and wore a black leather vest with multiple emblems on it. He was a very intimidating figure, but when he spoke, he had a soft voice and gave me the impression of a wise and gentle elder.

He introduced a group of indigenous people from California and Nevada who performed several ritual dances. It was an awe-inspiring presentation, and I was enamored with the power and grace of the mighty warriors who danced and chanted.

There were several other speeches and singing followed by an award ceremony. As I started to nod off, my father put his arm around me. At the end, the emcee gave an opportunity for people to speak and share thoughts about their loved ones. A few people volunteered and were handed a talking stick to share stories.

I was surprised when Mr. Moretti stood and asked to speak. As he walked to the stage, he was somber. It was a side of him I hadn't seen. Before he spoke, he stood quietly in front of everyone with a warm smile. The enormous fire silhouetted his figure and snapped behind him. He stood motionless, trying to find his words.

"I am so fortunate to be a part of this wonderful group and I thank you all for your support during these difficult times." He stopped and I could see his eyes watering.

"It seems we all take our lives for granted until something truly awful happens. Then we search to find some religious or spiritual meaning to help us through those difficult times. My wife always wanted me to be more religious than I am and drags me to church every Sunday." Several people chuckled.

"But I've come to realize we simply need to find our own religion whether in a god or in the stars or some power beyond this earth that can guide us." He choked back tears and stood quietly for a minute.

"My solace is that I have great friends and a truly beautiful family to help me through these times. I know our path forward in the coming months will be a difficult one and I thank you all so much for your prayers and support. Thank you." His eyes watered as he waved to the group and the large Indian chief embraced him in a hug.

I turned to my dad and could see him tearing up in the firelight. He gave me a hug and kissed me on the head. After the ceremony, our tribe quietly walked back to our cabins.

When we got back, Mr. Moretti clapped his hands and told a joke that made all the fathers start laughing. They started a fire and placed chairs around it in a circle, then carried out an enormous ice chest full of soft drinks and beer.

We roasted marshmallows, played games, and sang at our campfire until late into the evening. I ran endless circles around the campsite with the other boys until I collapsed in my father's lap. I was covered in dirt and sticky food when he put me into my bunk that night. The scent of Old Spice and Budweiser showered me as he brushed the hair from my face and kissed my forehead.

"I love you, Little Man," he whispered.

"I love you too." As he started to walk out, I yelled, "Dad?"

"Yes?"

"Why is Mr. Moretti so sad?"

He stood in the dark then slowly approached the edge of the bunk. "I think he is just worried about Michele. She is sick and he wants her to get better."

"When do you think she will get better? I miss seeing her."

"I don't know. It will take some time while the doctors give her medicine to make her better. Hopefully not too long."

I thought about what he said for a minute while he stood there staring at me. "She told me it's cancer. What if she doesn't ever get better?"

He was silent and I could hear him breathing through his mustache as he leaned against the bunk. "Yes, I suppose that's a possibility. But for now, let's just think about all the fun times we have had with Michele and hope the doctors can make her better. OK?"

"Yeah, I guess so."

"I love you, Little Man, get some sleep." He kissed me again then walked out.

As I lay on my back, I watched the stars, thinking about the speech Mr. Moretti gave. I thought about Michele's sickness and couldn't help but wonder what happened after this life. The stars glimmered brightly, millions of shining dots against a black quilt of endless space. I heard the fathers laughing around the fire as I drifted in and out of sleep, pondering an afterlife.

Later that night, I heard the low murmur of voices and scuffling in our cabin. I peered out the window. The fire had died to an orange glow. I could see several men scurrying by my window, carrying a long rectangular object out of our cabin into the moonlight. They placed the object just beyond the campfire then retreated to our cabin, chuckling. I was curious but rolled over and went back to sleep.

The next morning as the sun streamed through the large redwoods into our cabin, I was awakened by a rooster crowing. It sounded sick because the roosters' call was interspersed with a high-pitched cackle. I climbed down the ladder from my bunk and wandered out to the front room where my father was standing with several other fathers. They were looking out the front door and laughing hysterically.

They had carried out Mr. Moretti on his cot into the middle of our campground last night while he slept. He was laying on his back wearing nothing but boxer shorts and crowing like a rooster.

"Very funny, guys. Very funny," he said.

"That's what you get for snoring so loud," my dad responded.

"Yeah, well you guys better not go to sleep tonight."

My dad took multiple pictures of Mr. Moretti as he stood on his bed, posing in his boxer shorts.

— CHAPTER 10 —

Winning

The summers in San Jose were hot and most kids spent their days at the local swim club. Our club was called Los Ranchitos Banditos Swim Club and was located only three blocks from my house. It was the social hub of our neighborhood and provided a cool oasis in the heat of summer.

I could easily ride my bike there, so most days began with swim practice in the morning, followed by playing in the pool and lounging on the grass until late in the afternoon. I didn't leave until dusk when my mom told us to be home for dinner.

Weekends were dedicated to swim meets that lasted all day. My dad and Mr. Moretti managed the meets at our pool and seemed to enjoy the responsibility. Mr. Moretti would announce the events over a loudspeaker and my dad would manage the blocks and shoot the starting gun. They were both very entertaining and they periodically encouraged all the parents to spontaneously jump in the pool fully clothed.

Our swim meets were an interesting choreography of half naked kids buzzing around the circumference of the pool, while an intense group of adults screamed at the top of their lungs, cheering as their kids competed for sixty-second intervals. The irony was that most of the kids didn't really care about the competition in the pool. We just wanted to run around all day playing with our friends and shoving junk food down our gullets. I loved swim meets. On top of that, I was a decent swimmer and got to jump in the pool every once in a while to race.

One of our final competitions of the summer was held at the end of July. I raced my bike to the club in the morning and arrived just as an army of VW buses and wood-paneled station wagons pulled into the parking lot. Families started filing in with arms full of bags, towels, shade structures, ice chests, beach chairs and whatever equipment they required for a long day.

My parents arrived early in the morning to set things up and prepare for the meet. I ran in and found my mom, who was helping at the snack shack. She was mid-sentence, talking with a friend, and whipped out a black permanent pen from her back pocket. Without pausing her conversation, she began scrawling a bunch of information on the back of my right hand with the details of every race I was competing in. My coach had entered me in so many events that the black pen covered most of my hand and ran halfway down my arm.

My mom gave me final instructions and told me to pay attention to the announcer. She pointed to our allotted section of grass where there was an ice chest full of snacks, chairs and an umbrella. "You should go relax for a few minutes before your first race."

"Okay." I nodded.

As I ran over, I heard Mrs. Moretti call out. She was sitting in a chair next to our spot under a big blue umbrella with Michele. I hadn't seen Michele since our encounter at The Yardstick.

Ms. Moretti immediately embraced me with one of her hugs and I was engulfed in flowery perfume. She kissed me on the cheek and pointed to Michele who was sitting on a blanket under the umbrella.

"Look who's here." I was so happy to see her, but somewhat taken aback. She was swaddled in a blanket and her face was gaunt. She seemed much smaller and more feeble beneath her red bucket hat. Her brilliant green eyes beamed up at me and she was grinning.

She could tell I was apprehensive and held out her Paddington Bear. She asked me to sit down next to her on the blanket. I wasn't scared as much as I was concerned. It hadn't been until that moment that I grasped the full gravity of how sick she was. I carefully sat down beside her and patted Paddington.

"I'm so happy to see you," she said.

"Me too," I mumbled, unsure of myself. I didn't know what to say.

"Are you swimming a lot of events today?" she asked.

"Yes, coach has me in a ton." I was excited and held up my hand with all the black writing. "Are you going to watch?"

"Yes, of course, I can't wait," she said.

"What have you been doing this summer?" I regretted asking the question and felt bad for saying it.

"I spend a lot of time with my mom at our house. We bake sometimes and she has been showing me how to sew. The doctors say I should stay home and rest for most of this summer so I can get better."

I nodded and wasn't sure what to say. We sat quietly in an awkward silence. She seemed lonely and it felt like I was a million miles away from her. A group of other kids flitted around us, yelling and laughing. I wanted her to get up and run off with me to play.

She bumped Paddington Bear against my arm. "Hello?"

"Hi," I yelped.

She had a plastic container of coloring pens and asked me

to draw with her.

Her mom had been eavesdropping and quickly rummaged through a giant canvas bag to retrieve some paper for us to draw on. She handed us the paper then adjusted her sunglasses and turned away, pretending to watch the swim meet.

I sat coloring with Michele, laughing and enjoying her company, until a girl came by ringing a bell, announcing my event. Seeing how the disease had ravaged Michele's body made me sad, but sitting there, hearing Michele's voice and hearing her giggle, gave me a feeling of warmth. When I turned to say goodbye, her energetic eyes reminded me that my friend Michele was still here.

"I have to go to my next race." I patted her bear on the head and started to leave when she grabbed my wrist. She pulled my hand over and quickly scrawled a happy face on the back of my hand.

"Good luck! This will make you swim faster." I examined the drawing as I hopped up.

"Thanks."

"Swim fast. I will be cheering for you." She flashed a "thumbs up."

As I turned to run away, Mrs. Moretti said, "Good luck, Marky."

For the fifty-yard backstroke, I barely out-tagged another kid at the finish and there was a huge uproar on the deck. I thought I had done pretty well because Mr. Moretti made an excited announcement that I couldn't hear. As I bobbed in the pool, my dad grabbed my wrists and ripped my chubby little body from the water. He raised me triumphantly in the air and yelled something. Everyone was applauding and cheering for me.

"What happened Dad? Did I win?"

"Yes, you won! You broke the club record for backstroke by 1.2 seconds."

I was happy to win but didn't comprehend why it was such a big deal to break a record.

Throughout the day, I rotated between the pool to swim my events and the umbrella to spend time with Michele. Late in the afternoon, after I swam a relay, I went to share my results with Michele. When I ran to her umbrella, she and her mother were gone. There was a colorful drawing she had left under a rock on her blanket. It was a brilliant red flower bush with a bright yellow sun in the sky. Next to it was a caricature of a swimmer with a medal around his neck, holding one arm up. It was labeled "Mark" under the swimmer. I scanned the area to find her, but knew she had gone home to rest. I took the drawing back to my blanket and put it in one of our bags.

That night at the conclusion of the meet, there was a big awards ceremony. I was sitting in the middle of a large crowd as mostly older kids went up and received trophies and awards. I was awestruck at what amazing swimmers they were and the huge trophies they won.

My father and Mr. Moretti were presiding over the ceremony and I was talking with a friend when I heard my father announce my name. I looked up and he was holding an enormous trophy, staring at me.

"Mark Hober. Are you going to come up and get your trophy?" He waited, grinning at me and I thought he was joking.

"Is that for me?" I asked.

"Yes, get up here before we give it to somebody else."

There was a loud applause as I picked my way through the kids to the front. My dad held out the trophy. "Congratulations, Little Man. You are the Los Ranchitos Banditos record holder for the boys 8-10 backstroke."

I grabbed the trophy and could feel its weight in my hands. It had a shiny purple base and the figure of a powerful swimmer on top. I couldn't stop grinning. My dad hoisted my tanned little body in the air as everyone applauded and he kissed my cheek.

As we drove home that night and our VW banged along, I was transfixed on the massive purple trophy. I was proud but as I watched out the window at the stars, all I could think about was Michele. I wished she had been there so I could share it with her. I dug around in the bag to find the picture she had drawn, then pulled it out and flattened it on the seat. I felt an overpowering need to help her, however I could.

CHAPTER 11

What is Heaven?

The swim season ended in early August and we always celebrated with a blow-out party at our club to mark the end of summer. Historically, there had been a barbeque followed by skits performed by the kids and parents. However, my father had a penchant for always needing to make things bigger and grander. When he volunteered to take over the barbeque, he insisted on cooking a two-hundred-pound pig in the ancient Hawaiian style. This wasn't a small undertaking, and the amount of work and planning required to cook a pig was impressive.

The process began when he started digging a massive pit in the sandy area behind our pool. It took him almost two hours to dig the hole, flinging sand enthusiastically over his shoulder, sweating profusely from head to toe. He then filled the pit with large stones, which he heated in a fire that burned throughout the day. In the evening, he wrapped the pig in moist burlap sacks and banana leaves, then buried the pig in the ground with the hot stones to cook overnight.

He usually enlisted the help of several other fathers for this project and they would stay up all night telling stories and drinking beer. I had just turned eight that summer and he asked if I would like to help him. I was excited he asked me to help with such a big responsibility and agreed. I couldn't wait to stay up all night, telling stories and hanging out with my dad.

When he told me we needed to "go get the pig," I assumed we were just driving to the local grocery store. It never dawned on me where he actually procured the pig. It turned out the pig was on a farm almost two hours out of town where a rancher provided the beast in its entirety.

As we drove through the hills south of the city, I quickly fell asleep and didn't wake up until my dad tapped my leg. Our van was banging away, laboring to get up a steep gravel road. I watched as white fences and green pastures passed by the window. There were cows and horses grazing in the surrounding meadows and I could smell fresh cut hay and manure in the air.

"It's pretty out here, isn't it?" I rubbed my eyes and nodded, staring out the window.

"Where do they keep the pigs?" I asked.

"I'm not sure. I think they are in a pen behind the barn."

"You mean like a pig pen?"

"Yes, exactly!" He laughed.

The top of the gravel drive opened to a large courtyard surrounded by oak trees with an old barn on one end and a long, yellow ranch house on the other. My dad pulled halfway around the circle and stopped in front of the barn. There were massive wooden doors that had been partially rolled open.

"Do you want to come with me?" I was studying a group of the chickens wandering around, pecking at the ground.

"Sure." As I jumped out of the van, two men in overalls greeted us.

"Jim, it's great to see you. How have you been?" My dad spoke with the two men for a few minutes and then introduced me.

They looked down at me and winked. "Great to meet you,

Little Man."

"Are you helping your dad cook the pig?" one of them asked.

I grabbed my dad's leg. "Yep."

"He is my helper this year," my dad said with a grin.

"Well, that's great, it's a big project and your dad will need a lot of help. C'mon and I'll show you where your pig is. We just got her all wrapped up."

We followed the men back into a corner of the barn that was cleared out except for a massive steel table and sink. I half expected to see a pig on a leash that my father would simply walk out to our car.

The man pointed to a large four-wheeled cart that had a heap on top of it, swaddled in burlap sacks.

"Here she is. She weighs almost two hundred pounds after cleaning." There was red liquid dripping from one of the corners. The man whipped out a rag from his back pocket and wiped the corner.

"We'll go ahead and wheel her out to your van and help you get her into the back. You got help unloading her?"

My dad laughed and said, "Yes, definitely. As strong as Mark and I are, we will recruit some people to get the pig into the ground."

My face must have conveyed the disgust I was feeling as I watched them pushing the cart out toward our bus.

"Hey, Markle Farkle. Why don't you wait out by the chickens?"

I ran out to the big circular courtyard, happy to distance myself from the gruesome scene.

The chickens had all gone up to the front of the ranch house and were wandering around, pecking at the ground. As I followed them slowly around the courtyard, I stopped at a set of stairs that ran up to a long porch surrounding the house. There was an enormous oak door at the entry and a swinging chair hanging to the left of the door. On a wall beside the chair was a placard with a picture of a woman and writing that read, In loving memory of our mother and wife Pamela Hansen (1927-1974).

I stared at the message for several minutes, soaking in its full significance. I had seen signs like this before but usually at a church or cemetery. It seemed strange to see at a house where people were living.

"C'mon, Little Man, time to go," my dad said. I turned to see him shaking hands. He embraced one of the men for a moment then patted him gently on the shoulder. I heard him thank the men then say, "We will have you in our thoughts."

When I approached, the men both extended their hands to shake mine. "You seem pretty strong, Mark, be sure and help your dad with that beast. He'll need all the help he can get." They chuckled as I shook their hands.

My dad opened the passenger door and I hopped up into my seat. As my dad got in, he told the men, "I'll look forward to seeing you again next year." He started the car and waved at the men as we drove away. "Take care."

As we zig-zagged back down through the hills toward our house, I sat deep in thought. After twenty minutes, my dad asked me, "What are you thinking about?"

"I was just wondering what happens after people die."

My dad was outwardly surprised by the raw nature of my question. "Why are you thinking about that? Did the dead pig scare you?"

"Well…no. The pig was gross and everything but I saw a message on their house about a lady who died."

"What do you mean?"

"There was a woman's picture next to the swing on the deck and I think she died."

"Ooooh, I see."

He was quiet for a moment. "Well, that lady was married to one of those men, and she was the sister of the other man. Unfortunately, she got very sick and died this last year."

"She must have been really sick. Why didn't the doctors give her medicine to make her better?"

"Not all medicines work well enough to make people better. Sometimes a disease can get really bad and doctors can't fix it."

I pondered this for a minute. "So can anybody get a disease and die like she did?"

"She had a serious illness that doesn't happen to everyone. Usually when you get sick with a cold or the flu, the doctors can fix it. Her illness only happens to a few people."

"How do you think she got sick?"

"Well, you don't really catch it from other people like the flu. It's more like when something in your body just stops working the way it should. Like, you might not grow the way you're supposed to, or you can't heal from a cut or fight a cold."

"Did she have cancer?"

My dad was surprised. "Yes, it was a type of cancer called leukemia. How do you know what cancer is?"

"Because it's what Michele has."

"Did she tell you that?"

"Yes. She told me they are trying to help her get rid of it. It seems horrible and I want to help her."

My dad took a minute before answering. "It's good that you to want to help her, Little Man. She is a very special friend, and having a good friend like you right now is very important."

"What happens when you die?"

My dad was clearly not ready for this barrage of questions.

He wasn't a religious man but he was always very spiritual and gave this question a lot of thought.

"Well, some people think you go somewhere special after you die."

"Like heaven?"

"Yes, like heaven. A special place where everything is pleasant and it is very peaceful."

"Would I see Grandma and Grandpa if I die?"

"I suppose so, but I'd much rather you stay here with us for now." He patted my leg.

I stared out the window as the rolling hills passed by. Heaven sounded like a nice place and I envisioned what it was like, but it scared me to think of leaving my family and this life.

When we got back to the swim club, several of the fathers helped my dad lug the pig over to the giant hole. My mom gave us baloney sandwiches, which I enjoyed while they buried the pig in its burlap on top of the hot stones.

That evening, my father and I sat together in lawn chairs staring into the pit. The smell of roasting pork emanated from wisps of grey smoke. He played his guitar through the night, and we shared stories and laughed as he tried to recite the lyrics from various John Denver songs. I tried to stay awake but finally relented and passed out under a blanket in my chair.

As the sun began to rise the next morning, I awoke to the sound of my father spading dirt around the pit. He was maneuvering something in the ground to check the temperature of the pig. I sat up and enjoyed the purple sky. It was quiet except for a cluster of birds chirping in a nearby tree.

"How'd you sleep, Little Man?"

"Good." I yawned and stretched. "Is the pig still cooking under there?"

"Yep. Seems like it's getting there. Should be really good."

I rubbed my eyes and watched as the sky faded from light purple to a deep blue.

"Dad, do you think Michele is going to die?"

The interrogation of life after death and soul-searching queries can make any parent squirm. My dad believed in honesty but hesitated to expose me to the brutality of death at such a young age.

"I don't know. She is really sick and the doctors are doing everything they can to make her better. I think if we all think about her with 'good' thoughts, it will really help."

"Is that like praying?"

"Kind of. But you can also just think about the happy times you have had with Michele on our trips and at the swim club. She means a lot to you, so keep thinking about the fun times you have had with her."

The chair next to me creaked as my dad sat down and he placed the guitar on his lap. He looked in my eyes as I wiped tears away, trying to find happy thoughts for Michele. He leaned over, placing his forehead against mine.

"She is a very special girl, Mark. The doctors will do everything they can for her. In the meantime, let's think good thoughts and know she is loved." He squeezed my leg and smiled at me. "I've got a really good song I think you'll like."

As he began strumming his guitar, the sun started to warm my face and I could smell the pig roasting. I grinned as my dad crooned along next to me.

CHAPTER 12

Wishing on Stars

The best thing about our father being the Chief of our tribe was that we all got to wear impressive headdresses. Somehow my father had acquired beautiful head pieces that the chief and his son would don at each meeting or during campouts.

Unfortunately, we only had two headdresses. One for my father, and one for my brother and I to fight over. We alternated who got to wear it at each function but my brother managed to get himself disciplined, so my father said I would get to wear the chief's headdress at our next campout.

It was an amazing display of headwear and immediately commanded authority. A cluster of small feathers over the forehead exploded into a massive crown of blue, red and green shoots that stood two feet off my head. Flowing down the right and left lapels were beautiful banners of smaller feathers with similar green, red and blue flare interspersed by black feathers that screamed with power. I'm still baffled as to how my father acquired such a beautiful work of art for our little band of misfits.

I could barely contain my excitement when my father and Mr. Moretti announced that we were heading up to Lake Comanche for our end of summer camp out. I was beaming ear to ear, imagining all the Indian guides staring at my head-gear as I strutted through our campground.

My delusions came to a screeching halt when my dad announced that the "Y Indian Princesses" would be accompanying us for this final trip. The Princesses were the collection of little sisters in our tribe who were of appropriate age to periodically attend a campout. My hypothesis is one of the mothers finally cracked the code to our fathers' scheme and were told to bring the girls to one of the campouts.

"Girls are going to be there. Yuck!" I exclaimed.

As my dad packed the van for our trip, I was running in circles, anxious to hit the road. My brother sat pouting on the back seat since he would be relegated to wearing his standard headband.

I was buzzing around my father, giddy with anticipation, and reminded him at least five times to remember the chief's headgear. He finally went to his closet to retrieve the headdresses. He kept them on hangers in plastic sheaths to maintain their beauty. He ceremoniously carried them to the back of the van and hung them inside the rear door. I asked if we could wear them on the ride to Lake Comanche, to which my brother gave a dismissive snort. My dad reminded me we had to wait until that night's campfire to kick off the weekend's festivities.

I was dreaming for the entire drive up to Lake Comanche. When we finally arrived, I hopped out and sprinted to the nearest restroom. As I walked back to our campsite, I saw that the Morettis had arrived and parked their red VW van adjacent to ours. Mr. Moretti saw me and flashed his usual gregarious smile. He waved me over and was excited to share something.

"Mark, guess who's here?"

I stood dumbfounded because it seemed like a self-explanatory question.

"Um, I dunno?"

He waved for me to follow him to the side of their van. I had no idea what he was preparing to unveil. With a flourish of his hands, he pulled on the handle and slid the door open. Sitting quietly, swaddled in a soft blue blanket, was Michele. Her green eyes peered out from beneath a red headband with a single beautiful eagle's feather perched perfectly behind her head. I was elated to see her. It hadn't occurred to me that she might be there when our dads said the Princesses were joining us.

I looked at Mr. Moretti for permission to step inside. He nodded and said, "Go ahead, you can say hello."

She appeared very fragile and drawn. Her skin was a faded white color but her dimpled cheeks were flushed pink.

"I didn't know you were coming. I haven't seen you forever," I exclaimed.

She gave a faint smile and sat quietly examining my face for what seemed like an eternity. She craned her head to one side to see if her dad was still there, then I heard gravel crunching as he walked away.

"Yes, my dad wanted me to come. He said I would enjoy the fresh mountain air and stories by the campfire."

I pointed at the feather in her band. "That's a big feather. Did you earn it doing chores?"

"No, my dad gave it to me. He said I deserved it for everything I've been through. Plus, I can't really help with chores."

"What do you mean?"

She pulled my arm toward her and turned it over to expose the veins in the underside of my forearm. She stretched her arm out from beneath the blanket and showed me the blue veins running through her translucent white skin.

"The doctors say the cancer keeps my body from making blood the right way. It makes me really tired so I can't do chores."

I sat staring at her arm and the blue lines coursing blood beneath her skin.

"Why don't they just give you new blood?"

"I've gotten new blood but it only lasts for a little while."

I was perplexed. "Why?"

"I don't know. They are trying to fix my body to make blood the right way."

She became quiet and ran her hand up and down her arm squeamishly.

"They put needles in my arm and give me a lot of medicine through tubes."

I paused to confirm what she told me. "That sounds horrible," I said.

"Yes. I've kind of gotten used to it, but it hurts when they first put the needles in."

"That must hurt a lot."

"It does," she said in a whisper.

She didn't want to talk about it anymore. We sat staring at our outstretched arms. Her's was pale, fragile, and thin. Mine was tan and marked with blemishes from hours of four-square. She gently ran her hand up and down my arm.

"That tickles!" I said.

She chuckled and pushed my arm away.

I looked at the feather standing proudly behind her head. "That feather is beautiful. That has to be one of the biggest ones I've ever seen."

Michele reached up and brushed it. "Yes, it's really pretty. And soft."

"You should see the headdress I get to wear tonight. It's giant and has tons of different colored feathers. You'd really like it. I get to wear it because my dad is chief."

"I can't wait to see it."

"I'll show it to you tonight." I knew she would appreciate

the beautiful tapestry of feathers.

Just then, her dad came back and said, "Okay, pumpkin, I've got the tent all set up. You need to take a nap before tonight's campfire."

I turned to run out and for a moment, I thought she might follow me. I jumped down from their van and turned to see Michele's dad gently lifting her from the seat she was sitting on. She waved at me. I waved back then ran off behind our van to hide. I spied Michele as her father scooped her up from the bench.

It seemed wrong to run off and leave her there. Mr. Moretti ducked his head and walked carefully into their tent with his fragile bundle. He bent down and placed Michele on a cot, then knelt next to her. I could see him tucking blankets around her, then he kissed her forehead. He whispered to her, then removed the red band and feather from her head. It startled me because I had not noticed she was completely bald. Her smooth white head was almost blue in the sunlight and at that point, I fully realized that she was very ill.

I wasn't afraid for myself but for what might happen to Michele. I was overwhelmed with sadness and felt my stomach tense up. Everything slowed as I watched Mr. Moretti remove the lone eagle feather from its band and hand it to Michele. She ran her finger along it, then rotated it gently in the air. She ran it over her face, humming a song. Her father gave her a kiss on the forehead and stood to leave. I could hear Michele quietly singing as she waved the feather, conducting a silent orchestra.

As Mr. Moretti stooped to exit, he saw me watching from behind our car. He stopped for a moment and winked at me. I realized that I was crying and turned and ran toward our campsite.

It bothered me seeing her so sick and I wanted to bury the

thoughts and dark feelings. I quickly found a group of boys from our tribe playing kickball and joined in. I spent the rest of the afternoon running and playing, trying to forget about the sickness ravaging my best friend.

Night came as the sun slowly drifted behind the dry amber hills encircling Lake Comanche. My dad cooked a meal with some of the other fathers, bustling around a small green stove, then banged a fork on a tin cup and called for everyone to come eat. There were hot dogs, hamburgers, beans and a splatter of macaroni salad distributed to each boy on a metal plate. We huddled around a big wooden table sharing stories from the day's activities, eating our dinner and drinking canned soda. I tried not to think about Michele throughout the day, but she lingered in my thoughts.

As I finished dinner, I focused on the opening ceremonies for that evening when I could dawn the Chief's headdress. I jumped from the table and threw my metal plate in a tub of soapy water then ran to poke my dad who was deep in conversation. He held his hand up and told me not to interrupt. Of course, I continued to pull at him because the conversation seemed to go on indefinitely.

"What? I'm in the middle of a conversation."

I whispered in his ear with a final annoying plea. "When can we put on the headdress?"

He smirked and said, "Let us finish dinner and then we'll light the campfire."

"So how much longer?"

"I dunno, not too much longer. Go play with the other kids and I'll tell you when it's time."

I turned away and dragged my feet through the dirt toward the wooden table where some of the other boys were playing "Go Fish." I saw Liam sitting at the end of the table with his headband in his hands.

"Hey, what are you doing?" I asked. He was quiet and continued staring at his headband.

"I got two more feathers." He held the headband up for me to inspect.

"Wow, that's great," I said.

"How did you earn those?" I asked.

"Oh. Well, I just helped my mom wash some of the dishes and cleaned my room up. You were right, it is pretty easy to earn the feathers and they are really neat. I'll bet I can earn a hundred by next year." He put the headband on and started humming a song.

"What are you humming?" I asked.

"I dunno. I heard it on TV during an army show." He stood up and started marching around the table. All of the boys watched him with amusement as he hummed louder, circling the table. He laughed to himself then walked off into the darkness. I shrugged, then joined the boys in their card game.

As the cold began to creep in and the stars blinked to life in the sky, several of the boys gathered around the firepit with their vests on. Some of the dads placed a stack of wood in the firepit and ignited the base. Within minutes, a brilliant cluster of orange flames sprang from the cut logs, crackling and popping in the cool night air.

Mr. Moretti brought Michele out and set her in a giant beach chair, swaddled in blankets. She was beaming with her single eagle's feather proudly perched atop her head. Many people had begun collecting around the flames, holding their hands toward the heat. I didn't realize I had been staring blankly at Michele until my dad tapped my shoulder. He waved me toward the van.

"Are you ready?" A pulse of electricity pumped through my body.

"For the headdress!"

"Yep!"

"Yes! I can't wait!"

He slid the door to the van open and we pulled on our vests. Then he removed my headdress from its protective covering and placed it on my head. He unfurled the lapel banners and laid them down my chest. The weight of the crown and flowing tapestry ignited my excitement. I couldn't wait to strut around the fire in front of our tribe, especially Michele.

My father put on his own headdress, and I stood in awe. He looked powerful. I felt like we were superheroes, preparing to save the world.

He put his hand on my shoulder and said, "You are amazing, Little Deer."

I followed him as he walked out toward the campfire.

As we emerged into the light of the fire, all the chatter hushed.

Every person watched with admiration and respect. I pushed my chest out and stood proudly at attention as my dad kicked off the evening's events with a ceremonial speech. It was akin to a prayer that praised the practices and beliefs of the Chippewa tribe.

I don't remember a word he said. I stood there, soaking in the pride and admiration of all the kids seated around the fire. I remember Michele sitting close to her father and staring at me in my headdress.

The core activity of our ceremony entailed a "talking circle" where we would pass a talking stick and each person had an opportunity to share a recent story about something interesting or important in their life. The kids usually shared a highlight of recent sporting events on their soccer or swim team. The fathers would share an anecdote or funny story about work. Since my dad was the chief, he started that evening's talking circle.

As people passed the talking stick and shared their stories, I wore a grin from ear to ear, stroking the feathers flowing down my chest. My dad had to stop me on several occasions because there were balls of feather dander starting to build up on my pants.

When the talking stick got to Michele, her father laid it gently across her lap and I stared, waiting for her to share a story about her illness. There was a muffled silence around the circle as the fire popped and everyone focused on the pixie with a single feather standing proudly above her head. As she spoke, I felt a small tinge of electricity course through my body. Her brilliant green eyes sparkled as her gaze locked on me and it seemed as though just the two of us were sitting at the fire.

"I love laying on the grass watching the clouds in the sky and flying on my swing set, feeling the wind blow through my hair. I love seeing the flowers break through the soil and grow into beautiful colors. I love giving Paddington Bear hugs and playing with him and his friends. I love the smell of hot dogs at our swim meets and the pine trees when we camp." She paused for a moment and looked at me. "And I love my best friends for always making me laugh and helping me when I need it. Thank you for letting me join your campout!"

She passed the stick back to her dad and he kissed her on the head. "I love you, Waabigwan."

His eyes were watering as he struggled to tell the story of her name. It meant "flower" in Chippewa and he had given it to her because she was so beautiful and brought joy to everyone around her. The stories went on for another thirty minutes until the talking stick arrived back with my father. He concluded with another Native American prayer and thanked everyone for sharing.

As everyone began to disburse, Mr. Moretti stood to take

Michele to her tent. She was tired but still smiling. She tugged at his jacket and he bent over as she whispered something to him. He glanced at me as she motioned toward the woods. He shook his head at first, but she pulled his sleeve and was insistent. He finally relented and walked around the fire to where my dad and I sat. He whispered in my dad's ear, sharing the top-secret information she had discussed with him. My dad looked at me, then shrugged.

"Mark, Michele is very tired but she would like you to walk her down the path to see the river for a few minutes. Can you do that?"

"Why?" I said, confused by the request.

"I think she just wants to see the water and her dad said she likes to watch the stars."

I was nervous. It seemed odd and carried a tremendous responsibility.

"Why doesn't her dad just take her?"

Mr. Moretti cut in and said, "She asked for you to take her. I think she just wants to go with her good friend since this is a special trip and I always get to watch the stars with her."

I relished the idea of being able to spend time with Michele again, laughing and counting the stars. I looked across the fire at her and she crossed her arms, waiting impatiently. My dad nudged me.

"C'mon, Markle Farkle. It will only take you ten minutes and Michele would really appreciate it."

I stroked the feathers on my chest and he gently pulled my hand down.

"Okay..." I sprang to my feet and straightened the headdress. Most of the other kids had run off into the darkness and I could hear their voices echoing in the forest.

My dad went to our tent and retrieved a flashlight for us while Mr. Moretti imparted a litany of instructions to Michele and prepared her for the five-minute walk to the river. He put his down jacket on her and zipped it up to her chin, then put a beanie on her bare head. The headband didn't fit around the beanie so she insisted that he insert the feather in the back of her hat. When he had completed the preparations for our journey, she looked like a stuffed jacket with little legs and an antenna. Her hands weren't long enough to poke out of the sleeves so she cradled a flashlight in between her arms. My dad gave me a pullover sweater as well, but I demanded that I be allowed to wear the headdress on our adventure. He nodded at me with approval.

Our dads insisted we take a picture before departing so we squished together by the fire and awkwardly said "cheese" to my dad's 35mm Minolta.

As we marched off into the darkness, I could hear our dads chuckle as they barked, "Be careful!"

Our walk likely only took three minutes to the river but it seemed like an eternity.

We marched proudly by thousands of campfires and clusters of compatriot tribes as they watched with admiration. Michele rustled along by my side and grinned with pride. Thousands of eyes locked on us as we strode along the pathway, the Chief and Indian Princess. As we walked, I felt an uncontrollable energy that made me giggle

When we finally got down to the riverbank, we spotted a set of boulders to sit on. The moon was full and illuminated our path as we navigated our way down to the shoreline. The river chirped and gurgled as it bubbled through the forest from Lake Comanche on its way to the ocean.

Michele was tired and reached for me as we poked our way down to the boulders. She pushed her hand out through the bottom of her jacket and grabbed my hand. It was the first time I had held her hand. It surprised me. Her hand was warm and her touch jolted my core. My mouth suddenly locked shut from the flow of heat rushing throughout my body. I helped her down to the boulders and we sat studying the river as its black layers churned up white froth in the moonlight.

We held hands but didn't say anything. It was natural and I was thrilled to be there alone with her. She looked up at the stars and said, "I bet we can see a shooting star. My dad says they go by every two minutes. You just have to keep watching the sky to catch one."

I gulped and couldn't find the words.

"You need to make a wish when you see one," she said.

We both gazed at the night. There were thousands of stars in the sky. The river bubbled at our feet and the rich smell of redwood laced with ribbons of campfire permeated the cool mountain air. I smiled to myself, happy to be with her.

I don't remember if we ever saw a shooting star, but I do remember the wish I made. I glanced sideways to admire the joy in her face as she gazed skyward. The feather in her cap shone in the moonlight. She was so happy and full of life, it seemed hard to believe she was sick. I did everything I could in that one wish to make her better. I knew it would work. We held hands, watching for a shooting star for what seemed like hours.

When we finally decided to walk back to our campsite, Michele pulled my hand and demanded that I look at her. Her eyes watered as she whispered, "Sometimes I get scared. And sometimes I get mad or sad. I don't always know what I'm feeling and then I just get tired and take a nap. But I really like laughing and having fun with my friends, and my Paddington and my family ... and you. Thank you."

She held out her thumb as I sat speechless.

"Peep!"

I was trying not to cry and blurted, "peep." We laughed, then slowly made our way back to camp.

When we returned, all of the fathers were clustered around the campfire, laughing and reminiscing about a story someone was telling. When Mr. Moretti saw us, he didn't seem surprised or concerned. He simply gave us a bear hug and said, "thank you," then scooped Michele up in her stuffed jacket and took her back to their tent for bed.

I laid in my sleeping bag that night, listening to the fathers drinking beer and sharing stories as the campfire crackled in between their laughter. I couldn't sleep and was energized with thoughts of Michele and how happy she made me feel.

Later in the evening, the popping from the campfire woke me and I heard Mr. Moretti talking quietly. I struggled to hear what he said in a low whisper. It was about the medicine the doctors had been giving Michele, which didn't seem like it was helping. In fact, it just made her feel sicker. He said he and her mom didn't know if they wanted to take her to the hospital anymore. I was confused why they wouldn't take her to the hospital and thought maybe she was getting better. He wept for a few minutes while the other fathers expressed their gratitude for him.

— CHAPTER 13 —

Black and White

Late one afternoon in September, my mom knocked gently on my door and asked if she could come in. When she opened the door, I could tell something wasn't right. Her eyes were red and her voice trembled when she spoke. She was wearing an oversized grey sweater and seemed tired. She sat on the edge of my bed and took my hand in hers. Her hands were soft and smelled like roses.

"Dad and I are going over to the Moretti's for a short visit and we would like you to come with us."

At first, I was excited because I hadn't been over there in a long time. "Yes, I haven't been over there forever."

My mom was holding back tears and sniffled. "Mark, Michele won't be there, unfortunately."

I knew the answer to my question before I asked. I couldn't speak and my throat hurt when I uttered the words, "Did she die, mom?"

She didn't respond. She nodded and began crying as she pulled me close and wrapped me in a hug.

We held each other, crying for what seemed like an eternity. I felt a pang in my chest and began going through my never-ending list of questions again. Why couldn't the doctors help her? Why didn't the medicine work? Did it hurt when she died? What did she go through? Where is she now?

What is heaven like? What will it be like without her around anymore?

When my mom finally released me, she kissed my cheek and I asked if I could just lay down on my bed. She pulled a blanket over me and brushed the hair from my face.

My dad came in a few minutes later and patted my back.

"You awake, Little Man?"

"Yes. Is it really true, Dad?"

"Yes, I'm afraid so, Little Man. She was a very sweet girl and we will all miss her a lot."

"Why couldn't they help her?"

"I don't know. Sometimes they just can't fix what's wrong, no matter how hard they try."

"Do you think it hurt?"

"No, I don't think so. She probably just fell asleep quietly."

I imagined her falling asleep with Paddington bear under her arm. "She's in heaven now, right, Dad?"

"Yes, I'm sure she is, Little Man." He winked at me through teary eyes and pulled me in for a hug. "I love you, Little Man."

"Are we going over to the Moretti's now?"

"Yes, we just wanted to see her parents and give them hugs since they are probably very sad. They also wanted us to have a chance to say 'goodbye' to Michele."

"What do you mean?"

"We are going over to their house to talk and share nice thoughts about Michele. I think they would really like it if you came."

I thought about the invite for at least thirty minutes. My dad finally came back in my room and told me it was time to go. He didn't ask again. He just held out my coat and helped me put it on.

As I walked out into the family room, my brother was sitting on the couch next to my mother. It was odd because he didn't say a word. He just patted my back as I walked out with my father.

We were silent for the five-minute drive to the Moretti's and I peered out the window as the high pitch from the VW engine banged along. As we passed by a park, a group of Shakies had gathered in a circle below a grove of trees. They were singing together while someone played a guitar. I thought I saw the familiar cross and snake tattooed on one of the men's arms. He glanced toward us and flashed a peace sign. I waved as they disappeared into the distance.

When we arrived at the Morettis' house, the sun was just beginning to set, and the neighborhood was still. My dad rang the doorbell and we stood quietly waiting in the darkness of their entry. For those few minutes, I hoped it was all a mistake and Michele would answer the door.

When Mr. Moretti finally answered the door, he greeted us with open arms and invited us inside. Mrs. Moretti came into the entryway with Josh and we all exchanged hugs. It was quiet except for our sobs as we all moved around and embraced one another.

There was a picture of Michele on a table in the entryway. She was wearing a pretty white dress, beaming from ear to ear with her infectious smile. A vase of beautiful red mums sat next to her picture and smelled like spring.

Mrs. Moretti invited my mom and dad to the living room so the adults could visit. My brother and I followed Josh into the family room to watch TV. They sat next to each other on one end of the couch. I sat by myself on the other end. There were bowls of Chex mix and Cheetos on the coffee table. It was probably the first time I didn't feel the need to gorge myself on junk food.

The television was playing an old black-and-white re-run of Laurel and Hardy.

David and Josh watched the television in silence as I sat quietly inspecting the room. It was dark and the curtains were pulled close. The light from the TV cast shadows on the walls as I imagined Michele dancing around the room.

She was flitting about, running her hand over the table, making silly faces to see if she could make me laugh. She pretended to be a ballerina then did cartwheels across the carpet, ever the entertainer. We ate snacks from the bowls and threw the Cheetos at each other. She punched my arm and told me to catch her as she tore around the room, giggling.

We laid on the grass in her backyard and she told me stories about Paddington bear and her many global travels. We talked about the clouds in the sky and the birds as they flew by.

I sat in the dark, enjoying memories of Michele and pretending she was still there with me in her house. I eventually fell asleep on the couch until I felt my dad pick me up and place me over his shoulder to go home.

— CHAPTER 14 —

Saying Goodbye

That September on my first day of school, I arrived early as usual. I ran to the back of the school, shoved my bag lunch in a cubby, and sprinted out to the playground. The sun was just beginning to brighten the sky and wisps of steam rose from the blacktop.

I stopped to watch the foursquare competitions, then looked toward the big metal climbing structure standing in the shade. I knew what I needed to do and ran toward the back of the playground.

The birds were chirping in the early morning sun as I observed Michele's garden. The small white fence was leaning over in some areas and weeds had taken over. Most of the flowers had died but there were some vestiges of greenery in the sunlight.

I ran to the gardening shed and grabbed the trowel and bucket of tools she had placed on the shelf. I held the trowel in my hands for a moment and thought about Michele holding it in her hand, working in the garden.

I began pulling the weeds that had invaded the garden, then started turning the dirt over and spreading it out so water could get to the roots of the plants.

As I spade the dirt, a fat night crawler squirmed on the surface and tried to dig back into the soil. I laid down on my stomach, watching the worm. I envisioned Michele talking to the worm, prodding it to provide nutrients for her flowers.

I was jolted from my thoughts when I felt a kick on the back of my foot. I didn't need to turn to see who it was.

"Hey, Liam," I said, staring at the worm.

"What are you doing? Oooh, that's a big one. Let's cut him in half, I heard it will grow into two worms."

"No. They are good for the flowers and I'm taking care of the garden from now on."

"Okay, that makes sense." He laid down next to me as the worm burrowed into the earth.

"It sure was nice to have this garden here. It smelled really nice and all the flowers were pretty," he said.

"You wanna help me fix it up? You could use this as a project to earn another feather."

"Sure! What are we doing first?"

"Returning energy to the earth."

"What?"

"Cmon. Let's start by pulling out the rest of these weeds."

The Recurring Dream

I find myself standing at the edge of a beautiful green meadow that stretches to the hills in the distance. A cool breeze tosses the ocean of grass and sweeps over me as I breathe in its scent. It is a mixed fragrance of wheat tinged with fresh soil covered by the early morning dew.

The meadow is outlined by a geometric white fence that provides a sense of security in this expanse of beauty. It is an idyllic panorama that fills me with euphoria and heats my belly with excitement, drawing me inside. I pause, gripping the fence before entering the pasture, as I sense a danger lurking inside. Eventually, I release the post I am clinging to and am pulled inward, hands outstretched, soaring over the meadow, exhilarated by the beauty and innocence of this sacred place.

I fly back and forth above the soft tapestry, enjoying the freedom of flight, smiling and filled with a euphoric energy that keeps me aloft.

As I soar, I scan the horizon and see a glistening black shape that slowly comes into focus. The shape doesn't move but I can sense that it is a powerful creature which has known this pasture much longer than I. As I get closer, I begin to recognize the shape of the creature. It is a perfectly sculpted black bull standing proudly in the middle of the pasture. Its powerful muscles ripple beneath the sun and perfect ivory horns point in my direction.

I sense him studying my presence as I draw closer. His eyes pierce my interior and search deep into my soul. He delves into my thoughts, my fears, and knows my indiscretions.

His steel eyes judge me as I am dragged to his feet. As I attempt to change direction and flee, my body won't respond. I continue soaring toward him drawn by his gaze.

As the distance closes, I realize that he has rendered judgment and a deadening sensation of panic pumps throughout my body as I try to turn. I can hear a bellowed snorting as his hooves grind at the earth and tear against the green tapestry rushing toward me. My heart pounds and pushes hot iron through my veins. I claw at the air with weighted arms and feet to no avail.

The bull lowers his head as I brace for impact.

I am slammed in the abdomen and hurled into the sky. As I waft to the ground, the bull waits, then plunges both horns into my crumpled torso. He stands over my body, inspecting my hapless form splayed over his emerald dominion as crimson circles expand into my cotton shirt.

I don't feel any pain from the impact, but my fear fades to sadness as I leave my body. Floating above, I watch my crumpled silhouette and the bull drained of innocence is sniffing at its crime.

The bull's emotions pour into my consciousness as a deep sadness rises within him. He is conflicted with the need to remove this intruder from the sanctity of his kingdom versus the cost of that expulsion. The death of this young, innocent boy clings to his chest and he can't free himself of overwhelming guilt. His heart pounds heavily against his chest. Sadness engulfs him. I try to free myself from the bull's soul until I finally awake.

Mark Hober

Mark Hober has worked in the biopharmaceutical industry for over thirty years and has gained a deep appreciation for

the work being done by researchers around the world to find treatments for complex and rare diseases. He enjoys writing in his spare time and wrote his first two books, one for each of his daughters, on their sixteenth birthdays. Mark has a wonderful wife and two beautiful daughters who have encouraged and supported his writing pursuit over the years. When Mark isn't working, he enjoys the outdoors, traveling, mountain biking and hiking with his wife. They split their time between the San Francisco Bay Area and Bend, Oregon.